SHIFTING WORLDS

Darian Smith

TABLE OF CONTENTS

FOREWORD

Any experienced writer asked to judge a short story competition would probably confess they approach the task with a mixture of caution and trepidation. For every gem one reads, there are ten less shiny baubles that need polishing, cutting or simply throwing back into the grinder for some serious reworking.

Imagine my delight, if you can, in stumbling across the gem I was hoping for in a pile of rather ordinary entries into a writing competition I had been asked to judge. This was my first taste of Darian Smith. His intriguing mix of superpowers and Pasifika simplicity made his story stand out, head and shoulders above his competition.

I had no idea who Darian Smith was at the time. The entries were unmarked, so I couldn't tell anything about the author, other than he made me sit up and take notice. It is a delight to recognise one is reading the work of an author with true talent, rather than someone who simply wanted to write.

Darian continues to intrigue and delight me.

"Shifting Worlds" features stories from the realms of fantasy, sci-fi, and literary fiction. All of them challenge their protagonists by fundamentally altering their reality in some way. Whether the poignant personal touches of stories like *Atrophy*, *Spring* or *Seahorses*, the thought-provoking *The Girl in the Window,* the mischievous, *Cut and Colour*, the delightful *Drag Marks*, or the intriguing *Banshee*, Darian never fails to entertain and surprise the reader with his skill and his insight into to the human condition.

As a bonus, Darian offers a peek into his private world with a short explanation of his inspiration, motivation and sometimes raw, personal connection to each story, making you want to go back and read them again with the knowledge of what inspired it breathing new life into each story, doubling the reader's enjoyment with the benefit of this additional insight.

And then there is *A Suitor*, which begins: *It is my wedding night and I'm holding a knife stained with blood.* By far the best first line I have read in a long, long time.

This collection has it all. Honesty, insight, mischievousness. And fearlessness. It is also a great read.

I hope you will enjoy reading it as much I did, and maybe, if you're lucky, as much as Darian obviously did writing it.

Jennifer Fallon
Author of the Demon Child Trilogy, The Hythrun Chronicles, The Tide Lord Quadrilogy, The Second Sons Trilogy, The Rift Runners Trilogy and The War of the Gods Trilogy

INTRODUCTION

One of the most common things a writer gets asked is "Where do you get your ideas?"

Often, it's a question that's hard to answer. Inspiration can strike from nowhere. But sometimes it comes from something intensely personal - our fears, our darkness, our life experiences and strange thoughts. Our shadow self. Artists of all kinds have a long-standing reputation for being tortured, sensitive types, dancing close to madness to release their creativity. And with good reason. Art requires truth. No matter how fictional, a good story, one that resonates, has some kernel of truth.

That truth could be about emotion, about society, about humanity as a whole, or about ourselves. Stories are often a way to process an emotion or experience – to extrapolate it to a fuller conclusion in a way we wouldn't dare do in real life. They are literally (and literature-ly) where the author's demons hide.

The stories in this collection are a mix of speculative and literary fiction. Some have been published elsewhere and some have won prizes. Others are new or previously unseen favourites. They all shift the world in some way for the characters inside them.

After each one is a short note on the origin and inspiration behind the story.

I hope you enjoy them.

Darian Smith

WEARING THE STAR CLOAK

There's a moment, just before waking, when I forget it's gone. I feel the ghost of it on my shoulders, the warmth inside. It boosts my confidence and makes me stronger. I am more myself. I am ready to rule the islands and mould the day to my bidding.

Opening my eyes is a disappointment. My old bones ache with craving. It's been missing from me for almost three decades, but I feel it just the same. I'm simply an old man with his memories and regrets. I had my chance. I was not worthy.

The woven flax that covers my doorway is brushed aside to reveal the antidote to my thoughts. Iolani smiles like the last of the sun glinting off the dark ocean at twilight. They say that our children and grandchildren are our greatest treasure. Iolani is mine.

"Good morning, Grandpa. I brought you breakfast." She lays a tray lined with banana leaves beside my sleeping mat. It is covered in sliced pawpaw, banana and coconut.

"You're a good girl."

Her eyes dance and her smile gets even wider, then her face twitches and the smile disappears.

"What is it?"

She shakes her head. "Nothing, Grandpa. Enjoy your breakfast."

I roll quickly to my feet and tug the flax mat covering the window away. Sunlight fills the bure. Iolani turns as though to leave, but there's speed in my old bones yet. I grasp her by the shoulders and turn her to face me, peering closer. In the corner of her lip, there is a smudge of blood. "Who did that?"

She shrugs. "Kaha's brothers, of course. He's been the Anela for a long time now so they think they're untouchable."

"And are they right?"

The other corner of her mouth twitches upwards. "The one with the bruised coconuts wasn't."

I laugh. "I hope you kicked him good and hard!"

She tilts her head and looks up from under innocent eyelashes. "I may have. He made me spill the milk I had on your tray."

I find my laugher has gone. "This happened just now?" I frown at the doorway. "On the way here?"

"Yes, but..."

I'm already striding past her, breakfast forgotten. The flax in the doorway is like mist to me. Outside, the sun beats down through the coconut palms, shining brightly coloured on the hibiscus around my home. Four boys are waiting, loitering amongst the tree trunk shadows like eels preying on unwary fish. They're around Iolani's age.

"You don't belong here," I call out. "Get moving."

7

Two of them shift as if to obey, but the other two hold their ground. "Fuck off, old man. We don't have to do what you say."

"You do if you don't want me to summon the Elders and tell them you've been bullying women."

The ringleader lifts his chin. "Do it. I'll call Kaha'aheo. The Anela beats the Elders."

I stare him in the eye. It is a gaze that quailed enemies in earlier days. Respect fades with power, it seems. "Your brother won't wear the Whetu Korowai forever."

"Oh yeah? Want me to summon him now so you can say that to his face?"

I shrug. "Summon him if you wish. Tell him I will meet him in the choosing circle." No Anela ever returned to the choosing circle willingly. It was too harsh a reminder of what happened to most of them. It'd taken me years before I could face it again.

The boy shifts uneasily. "Whatever. Let's get out of here." His brothers move with him, a beast with four heads. They will be back, I'm sure. The fifth brother, the one who wears the star cloak, gives them confidence. He lends them power by association. Power corrupts. I should know.

Iolani waits in the doorway to my bure. The smile is back, although it must hurt her lip to do it. "You're awesome, Grandpa." She throws her arms around me.

The smile is infectious. "Hardly."

"No, it's true. I can just imagine what you were like when you wore the Whetu Korowai. The way you used the magic to defeat the Maloan Islanders. If I ever get the chance to be the Anela, I want to be just like you."

8

She intends it as a compliment, but when Iolani leaves, her words haunt me. My time in the Whetu Korowai made me a hero to the people and left me with nightmares.

The Maloans had competed for fish in our waters and sometimes their young men would come looking for wives. We would fight them, pushing them back to their own island so we could coexist.

The last time they'd done it, I was new to the star cloak. I believed conquering enemies was a worthy use of the power. I pulled a storm from far out to sea and set it over their island where it raged for five days. When it was over, I led the warriors to finish off our enemy.

The village was like a crab crushed between two rocks. Pieces of broken homes floated in a goo of mud, sticks and blood. Drowned corpses stared at us with bloated faces as the few survivors tried to salvage what they could. When they saw us coming, they cheered, thinking we would be their saviours. Instead, we killed and raped. Our canoes were so laden with pillaged treasure on the way back, I had to use my powers to keep them afloat.

I'd earned the title of conqueror. It wasn't until later, when I looked back, trying to find reasons for my loss, that I realised the horror of what I had done. Of what I'd allowed to be done. My chance to prove myself worthy had come too early in life, before I'd learned what true worth was.

The melancholy stays with me all day and I keep mostly to myself, searching the rock pools for crabs and trapped fish to bring back home. There are more pools now than there used to be. When Kaha'aheo first became the Anela, he amused himself by blasting holes in the rock. The resulting benefit to food gathering was unplanned, but welcome.

The slow, soft brush of waves against the shore marks time until night falls and I leave my basket of collected food at my bure, then make my way to the choosing circle. A few of us gather there every evening to check for the stars' return. I'm barely half way there when I hear the drums.

They have come.

Rough flax, hibiscus and spiky grasses scratch at my legs as I hurry through the scrub. Even now, thirty years beyond being a candidate, the excitement builds in my chest. Iolani is old enough to put herself forward.

My old legs are not as fast as they once were. People have already gathered by the time I arrive. The circle is in fact an oval of hard-packed earth, pressed down by generations of feet. Hollowed half-logs form seats around the edges for those of us tired from the day. The rest stand behind, leaving the circle itself for those who would put themselves forward to wear the Whetu Korowai. At the far, narrow end, three standing stones rise tall and thin above us all. At the top of each is a hole through which one of the coloured stars can be seen. They have aligned once more. It is time for the choosing.

Iolani is among the young people waiting in the circle. The boys who bullied her are there too. She meets my eye and grins, bouncing slightly on the balls of her feet.

The chief stands and the crowd falls silent. "Since the time of the great leader, Haunani, we have seen many young people come forward to prove themselves worthy of his power, the Whetu Korowai. Yet none have kept it. Today, another will be chosen to show their worth."

"No!" It is an anguished cry that pulls at my core. The same cry was ripped from my own throat when the star cloak left me for another. I have heard it many times since then. The stars return to the standing stones every one to three years to choose another Anela. None have proven any more worthy than I did.

Kaha'aheo is fighting it. The crowd parts and I can see him at the edge of the clearing. His arms are wrapped around the trunk of a coconut tree as he tries to resist the inexorable pull back to the standing stones. The Whetu Korowai flutters from his shoulders, streaming like a waterfall of light. It is made of glowing, many-coloured feathers, insubstantial as mist, stronger than stone. As we watch, the feathers grow longer, like fingers, and the cloak bends, wrapping itself around him, pulling his arms away from the tree.

He cries out again, but it is too late. The light of the Whetu Korowai completely envelops him like a glowing cocoon. It floats slowly through the air, past the crowd, toward the circle. As it passes, I hear his sobs from within.

When it reaches the stones, the star cloak unravels and the old Anela is dumped on the dirt. His face is streaked with tears and he reaches toward the magic he has worn for almost two years. It dissolves, and the feathers of light spin up, through the holes in the standing stones and back to the stars.

"Sorry, Kaha." The chief speaks again. "All those

who would show themselves worthy to wear Haunani's magic should present themselves now."

Iolani and the others spread out in front of the standing stones, each vying for a position. The stars pulse and the light feathers flood back through the holes in the stone, returning to earth again. They swirl like a swarm of phosphorescent butterflies, swooping around and over the assembled youth.

I hold my breath.

The lights begin to coalesce back into the cloak. Kaha'aheo scrambles to his feet and tries to grab it for himself once more. There is a pulse and he is knocked backward, off his feet.

The feathers ruffle as though in wind. The cloak hovers near Iolani, then swirls around the ringleader of the bullies. My teeth dig into my lower lip. With the power of the Whetu Korowai that boy would be the worst kind of tyrant. A smile begins to form on his lips, then, with a twitch, the cloak flicks away, settling itself around Iolani's shoulders. The light flows into her and around her. Her hair and clothes and the feathers of the star cloak shift in the unfelt wind. There is a pulse of light, and it is done.

The three stars move out of position in the standing stones and continue their passage across the sky.

I clap my hands together. "Iolani! It's you!" My granddaughter is the new Anela. It is bittersweet that I cannot have the Whetu Korowai back, but at least my beloved Iolani can. I pray she can keep it and not have to suffer the way I did. The way Kaha'aheo now suffers.

The boy sobs. He is on his knees, his hands clawing at the dirt. One of his brothers goes to his side and puts a hand on his shoulder. The others seem lost.

I gesture to Iolani. She can afford to be gracious. Perhaps she can offer the boy a token to ease his loss.

She turns to him. "Shut up," she says. She flicks her hand and his body snaps back, spinning into the crowd.

"Iolani!"

Her face is hard. "What? He deserves it. You think he was being nice when he used to explode the rock around me, down at the beach? Not so funny now, is it? Look, I can do it too." A section of the earth next to her explodes outward, showering the crowd with dirt. There are screams.

Though I am unharmed, I feel as if it is my insides that are being pelted with tiny pebbles. My Iolani could not be corrupted so soon. "Iolani, please. You must remember to be worthy. This isn't the way."

She shakes her head. "You're wrong, Grandfather. Strength is worthy. You taught me that. You wiped out the Maloans to stop them harming our people. I will take it further and wipe out those of us who would harm each other."

She turns to the ringleader of the bullies, Kaha'aheo's brother. His eyes are wide. His lip trembles. He stands firm.

"Stand very still," Iolani says. She gestures with her fist and the ground beneath him erupts with the force of a storm. Brown and red geyser upward, then fall like hail and rain. His body lands twisted and broken. He is dead.

Iolani licks her lip where the blood was this morning. It is healed.

People jostle each other as they run. Others are rooted to the spot like a coconut palm - able to do nothing but sway in the wind.

My hands cover my mouth as I murmur my granddaughter's name into my palms. "Iolani. What have you done?"

"What needs doing, Grandpa. And I've just gotten started." The other bullies try to run but an invisible wall boxes them in. Iolani smiles an unpleasant smile. "Not so fun when you're not the one with the power, is it?" She lifts her hand and lightning crackles around her fingers.

"Stop this," I say, my words almost a sob. "Please. It isn't right!" I see the bloated faces of dead Maloans in the broken form of the dead boy. Iolani is going to be just like me. *Worse* than me.

"Yes," she says. "It is."

Her hand raises toward the boys and I move faster than I have in years. I fling myself between my granddaughter and her tormentors. The lightning strikes me in the chest and face. The world explodes in colourful feathers of light, then everything is still and dark.

It is a deeper darkness than night. A quieter stillness than the calm sea at dawn. It is the feeling of death and I make my peace. I have done what I can.

There is a shimmer in the dark, a pinpoint of light like the first tip of colour emerging from a hibiscus bud. It brightens and shifts like a firefly. Another joins it. And another. They circle around me, three stars, swirling, testing, observing. Then they speak, their voices like the distant chiming of delicate bells.

"This one has strength."

"And empathy. It knows loss."

"Sacrifice. And honour."

I can only stare, wordless.

"At last," they say, "the Anela has served its purpose. We have found one willing to stand against the power for the sake of another. He is worthy."

The stars grow brighter, merging into one. Then they merge with me and the world fills with light.

There is a moment, just before waking, when I forget that it is with me. When the memory of my regrets crumbles the strength in my bones and I cry with the need to help my people. I crave a chance for redemption. To calm the hatreds, restore the family bonds, nurture the sea and nourish the land.

I open my eyes to see stars beneath my skin. The Whetu Korowai is no more. Its power is part of me. I am Haunani reborn.

I've always loved the idea of having magical abilities or super powers but what if power really does corrupt? What if it corrupted me and I proved unworthy? Could I cope with that knowledge about myself? What would that mean? And how would a person deal with the loss of such power and self-belief?

The ideas in this story sat in the back of my mind for quite some time. I wanted to demonstrate a sense of regret and withdrawal as well as the wisdom that comes from making a huge mistake and learning from it.

It wasn't until SpecFicNZ and Wilywriters.com joined forces to hold a short story competition that I actually sat down to write it, giving it a Pasifika feel. The story won the competition and was later a finalist for the Sir Julius Vogel Awards.

ATROPHY

When I dream, Chrissy is standing. She drops a snowboard between us and points to the bindings. "Slide your feet in from the back. It's rear entry."

I raise my eyebrows. "Really?"

She gives me the trying-not-to-laugh look. "You want me to help or you want to be a smart-arse?"

"No no," I spread my hands innocently. "By all means, tell me about your rear."

She laughs for real then, and waits until my feet are locked in place, before standing very close, our lips almost touching. "I think you'll be seeing a lot of my rear as you try to keep up." She gives me a gentle shove in the middle of my chest, tipping me until I begin to topple. Before I can fall, she takes my hand.

We're moving together, Chrissy towing me effortlessly across a landscape of white. The scent of snow and pine flows around us like breath. The warmth of her hand seeps through my glove. I am happy. "Where are we going?" I ask.

"To the doctor."

My hand grows cold and she is suddenly nowhere to be seen. I am alone.

I wake up on the couch. The baby monitor we've been using as an intercom is silent. I walk to the bedroom anyway to check on Chrissy. Sleeping, with her body hidden beneath the covers, I can almost believe she is her old self again. I think about getting into bed with her but it's easier not to break the spell. I go back to the couch and lay down.

*

"There are limits," Kim says.

They're the same words the doctor used all those months ago. His image perches in my mind like some useless, white-winged bird amongst the evergreen décor of his office. "There are limits to what medical science can do," he'd said. "I'm sorry."

Kim grasps my shoulder and shakes the memory from its roost. "Hey," she says, "there are limits to what you can do, Dave. You need to give yourself a break. Come to the snow next weekend."

I take a slow breath of stagnant air and lean back against the kitchen bench. My hand traces idly over the special bread knife with the wide, perpendicular handle. Its blade slides through crusts like soft snow. Chrissy can't even use the special utensils any more.

"I'm fine," I say, putting on the polite thank-you smile. "Anyway, I'm so out of practice, I don't think I even remember how any more."

"Nonsense! It's like riding a bike, isn't it, Chrissy?" Kim picks up the plastic mug of tea and takes it across to my wife.

The setting sun sprinkles golden light over Chrissy's

face as she smiles. "Of course it is. You never forget how to ski. I assume." Her gesture takes in the wheelchair.

I try to smile at her attempt at humour. There's a long pause and the sun sinks away into dusk.

"You should go," she says later, as I'm lifting her into bed. "You don't see the old gang nearly enough any more."

I pull back the duvet, careful to cover where the pretty stitching she loves has worn through. "You don't see them either. Even Kim hardly visits now."

Her face twists. "Yeah, but there's a reason for that."

I sigh and sit on the edge of the bed for a moment, taking her hand. "People...don't know how to deal with it."

She squeezes my hand – so weak. "No kidding. But that's no reason for us both to miss out."

"I guess." I scoop her up and place her in bed. Her wasted limbs feel wrong to the touch, like soft leather pulled over bones. The healthy athlete I married now frail sticks on a stump torso. I fix my eyes on her face and my mind on how she looked when we met – long, sexy legs and a curved, capable body, seducing me away from skis with her love of snowboarding. Love is blind to imperfection. It isn't revolted by a ravaged body or dismayed by the physical progression of disease. Those are the rules.

I kiss her on the forehead, pull up the duvet and turn out the light before slipping in beside her.

"I'll get Mum or the respite nurse to take care of me that weekend," she says. "You should go."

*

The air is crisp and free, blowing in my face as I slide down the slope. Laughter bubbles up in me and I'm grinning like an idiot when I stop at the bottom in a spray of feathery snow.

Kim is waiting for me at the chair lift. "I'm glad you came," she says. "It seems like you needed it."

I nod, luxuriating in the icy cold. "I'd forgotten how much fun this is. There's nothing like it!"

"That's for sure."

The lift comes and scoops up the front two people in the queue. Kim shuffles forward but her skis cross and she loses balance. I catch her as she falls - her body is firm and rounded beneath her ski gear. She smiles as I tip her back onto her feet and gestures to my snowboard.

"All these years and I still cross skis! Maybe I should get one of those. You wanna give me a lesson later?"

I shrug. "Sure."

*

The hotel duvet looks new, pressed and pristine, despite its dishevelment. Kim stretches naked across it, her body so different to Chrissy's. I trace the curve of her bicep, fascinated by its roundness. She smiles. "Are you okay?" she asks.

"Yeah." I pull my hand away. "Sorry I finished so fast. It's...been a long time since Chrissy and I..."

"It's fine," she assures me. "It must be hard dealing with everything at home."

I stay quiet for a long time, staring at the abandoned pile of clothes and gear in the corner. "You know, when she first started losing her balance, I thought she was imagining it. Or maybe that she had an inner ear infection. I was so angry when she cancelled a ski trip to see the neurologist."

Kim flexes and twists her body to look at me. "There's no way you could've known. I mean, who thinks their muscles are going to just up and waste away?"

I roll onto my back and cover my eyes with my hand. "Yeah."

I can feel Kim's touch on my shoulder. "Hey, you're amazing. I honestly don't know how you can stay and deal with it for so long."

I stay silent. I don't know what to say.

"Well," she says, climbing astride me once more with her whole, muscular legs, "at least I can distract you for a little while."

*

"I'm glad you're getting back into the ski trips," Chrissy says as I thumb through the mail. "You seem more relaxed."

I keep my eyes on the envelopes. "Yeah. It's good to get out of the house now and then." There's a bill in the pile – we're late with the electricity again – and something from the DHB. That'll be another half day wasted in waiting rooms so someone can examine Chrissy and remind us nothing can be done. Sandwiched between them is the assortment of junk mail. Once we would have thrown this away, but Chrissy likes to read it now.

"I wish I could come," she says. "I miss the snow."

Between the Warehouse flyer and a makeup catalogue, there's a letter addressed to me. I recognise the company logo. I hand Chrissy her junk mail and the DHB letter, but keep the others myself. I take a deep breath and tear open the letter

"We regret to inform you..." The expected words jump out at me. "We can no longer hold your job open ..." The letter trembles.

Chrissy looks up. "What's that, hon?"

I put on a smile for her. "Some news from the office. No biggie."

She nods and goes back to reading her catalogues. Her head lolls slightly to the side. It's the third time I've noticed it this week. She sees me looking and carefully straightens up.

"Tired?" I ask.

She half shrugs. "A little."

She naps the rest of the afternoon. When the homecare nurse comes, I slip away.

Kim's apartment has an artsy feel to it with an easel with a half-finished canvas in the corner. Her gym bag and squash racquet are by the door.

"How about I make you a coffee?" she says, leading the way to the kitchen.

I sink onto a stool gratefully and watch her fill the kettle, open the jar of coffee grounds, and spoon some into the plunger. "You're fantastic."

She laughs. "For making coffee? Gee, you're easy to please."

Her laughter infects me, and I grin. "I guess I am. When can we get away again?"

"Soon, I hope. I'm thinking the weekend after next. How are you doing?"

I take a deep breath. "Chrissy's worse. She wet the

bed last night." I can still feel the dampness on my thigh.

Kim sets the milk down hard. "Oh God. I had no idea it would get that bad."

I stare at the dishes in the drying rack. They're all straight handled knives and regular utensils.

Kim touches my arm. "Hey." She hands me my cup.

"Thanks."

Her touch lingers. "You could just leave it all behind you know. We could go live at the mountain and teach snowboarding to tourists." She smiles as if she might be teasing, but it falters when I meet her eyes.

I drink the coffee.

*

I sit in the shelter of the bus depot, jacket zipped tight over dark jeans and a woollen jumper, just barely out of reach of the drizzling rain. The wind howls like a siren around the jutting glass cover. An abandoned newspaper separates, one page soaring into the sky, the other tumbling, broken, along the path to rest against my suitcase. It's the large suitcase. The serious one. My snowboard sits next to it. I have everything I need.

My chest feels bruised and tight. Chrissy flickers in my memory. "You should go," she says.

Soon she'll realise what I've done. She'll understand. There are limits to what a person can do. Everyone has limits.

The couple next to me huddle close, giggling as the rain sweeps towards them. Their skis are propped against backpacks with foreign language messages scrawled on them in permanent marker. They have matching jackets. Further along, a harangued woman with greying hair wrangles a group of teenagers on a school trip to the snow.

I turn the bus ticket over and over in my hands. By now, Kim will have arrived at our new flat and be unpacking. We agreed she would bring all of her things and I'd leave everything for Chrissy. It occurs to me that I should've brought my Nirvana CD. Chrissy never really liked it anyway.

The matching lovers tussle with an umbrella, trying to angle it to protect them both. The man moves to make room and his shoulder is quickly soaked.

The rain gets heavier, a grey veil pulled over the world. It obliterates everything.

The headlights of the bus appear, pushing through the grey to pull up in front of me. The door hisses open. The bags are hurriedly stashed and passengers climb aboard. The travelling couple are efficient and the teens enthusiastic. They want the journey to start.

The ticket feels rough against my fingers as the bus drives away. I let it slip into the wind and step out into the rain.

When my wife was diagnosed with muscular dystrophy, I was faced with the question that strikes the partner of anyone who acquires a serious illness or disability. It's not a nice question and we don't like to acknowledge it much, but it's there. The question is: Am I going to stay for this, or leave to build a "normal" life elsewhere?

It's a question which comes loaded with judgements. What kind of person am I? Can I cope with this? What does it mean for the future we had intended?

For me, the question was quickly resolved, but the shock of it means I'm much slower to judge others dealing with similar situations. Life can be tough and sometimes it's more than we think we can handle.

For me, "Atrophy" was a way to explore those feelings in more depth than reality allowed and process for myself what the outcome might have been if I'd chosen differently.

I entered the story in the Western Districts Short Story competition where it placed as Very Highly Commended.

The Girl in the Window

When my RAL scores had me assessed for archaeology, I felt like the air was pulled from my lungs. The past was a wasteland with no e-lens, no Relion helpers, and only one planet. Who would want to spend their life looking at that? I didn't understand the value of what we could do until later, during the war.

I was sent to help investigate the Nazca lines in Old Peru, Earth - huge geometric designs, stylised animals and figures carved into the desert, many kilometres long.

"This is the best job in the universe because we get to bring history back to life," Lara, the team manager, told me when I arrived. She had her e-lens set to chime every hour to keep her on schedule. "These patterns can only be seen from the air and we don't know how the ancient Nazca people could have built them. So we're keen to find anything that shows how they did it, or why." She paused and widened her eyes for effect. "They vanished after they finished the lines, you know."

I didn't care. Trying to focus a temporal window on anything of interest in a desert was not my idea of fun.

No one had lived there in centuries and I could see why. Time after time I resolved the window on barren dirt, hot stones, and nothing else.

Sure, the lines themselves were often seen in much clearer resolution. Peeling back the time layers let me see them as they'd been intended - a kind of giant, runic crossword spread across the country's landscape - but their meaning was always elusive and, without that, they were simply drawings that could be seen from the air. Dull drawings.

Being historians, my team quickly taught me the time-honoured ways to deal with boredom: drinking and sex. That, and e-lens headlines were the only things that kept me sane. It was there that the first hints of a Relion attack were released. I shrugged it off. Their sector was a long way away and, other than sharing their helper robot technology, they had little to do with us.

That day was also the first time I glimpsed the girl. When my randomly-plotted temporal window resolved, she was simply standing there, gazing over the desert scrub. Her body was sheathed in richly colourful and patterned fabric; her hair was long and black. In one hand, she held a round grey stone. In the other, what looked to be a dried human head.

My hand trembled on the controls. This, surely, was one of the people who'd made the lines. I flicked the switch for recording and tried to pin the coordinates in place. The girl turned and looked directly at me through the window, as if she knew I was there. When her gaze met mine, I twitched in reflex and the window collapsed.

I told Lara about it in bed that night as we caught our breath.

"That's good," she said, a wisp of blond hair with blue tips trailing across her collarbone. She shifted to look at me. "Now is definitely the time to show that we're making progress."

"Why's that?"

She chewed her lip a moment. "War is coming. That means changes in funding priorities."

"War?"

She sighed. "Apparently the Relions have been active for a long time. They're just starting to let the public know, but we're at war. We'll need to focus on finding something to give our side the edge."

I sat up, the covers falling around me. "Us? How?"

Lara looked at me, her brow crinkled. "Information, forgotten technology, lost mystical items or abilities. Anything that could be used as a weapon, really. So, Corin, what do you think the Nazca lines were used for?"

At the team meeting next morning, while Lara made the announcement about the war, I was thinking about the Nazca girl. The memory of her dark eyes looking right at me made it difficult to focus on anything else. Her clothing was from the era when the lines had been made. Add the fact that she'd been holding a stone when I saw her and she was an incredible find. I had to locate her again!

I practically lived in the dig-lab that week. I fiddled with the temporal resonance, I checked and rechecked the coordinates, I focussed the image so hard I saw spots in front of my eyes. I reprogrammed three Relion helpers to focus exclusively on my tech. The read-out displays on their egg-heads swirled like a galaxy storm.

Nothing worked.

I replayed the recorded image over and over, trying to catch a glimpse of some clue that would help me reset a window on her or her people. Every time, it seemed her eyes would watch me. Dark, warm eyes, with no hint of e-lens silver.

I was playing it again when I noticed something. The fabric the girl was wearing was woven with a familiar pattern. I pulled up a stack of images on my e-lens. Sure enough, there it was. The condor, one of the patterns created by the lines.

Lara looked up with a start when I opened the door of her office. Two men in military uniform sat in front of her desk with folders in their hands.

"I need to move my dig site to the Condor," I told her. "I think she's there."

"Fine." She made a sideways motion with two fingers. "Close the door."

In the new location, the temporal window resolved almost immediately on the Nazca girl. She was with her tribe as they worked to clear stones and dirt from a path marked with wooden stakes and twine.

She scraped at the ground with a wooden spade, digging up embedded rocks and throwing them into a basket. When it was full, she stood and stretched, her arching back pointing her breasts to the sun. The others kept working, but she turned slowly, as though seeking out the temporal window – seeking me.

She left the basket where it was and moved unerringly towards the spot where the invisible window opened. This time there was no mistaking it. She saw.

Her black hair spilled like glossy syrup, framing her

face as she looked at me again, dark eyes catching mine. "You came," she said.

A light switched on inside me. "Of course, I did."

She smiled and lifted a finger to her lips. "Ssshh. We don't have time now. They're here. Find me again tonight."

"Who's here?"

She pointed to something beyond the view of the temporal window. "Find me tonight. I am Chali."

The window closed, leaving me trembling. She had *talked* to me. I was sure she had. How was that possible? A temporal window only existed in one direction. It wasn't possible for the observed to know it existed. She shouldn't have even known I was there.

That night, I slept alone. When Lara's personal code flashed up on my e-lens, I ignored it. She was too professional to use her managerial code for a booty-call and, unless she did, I was under no obligation to answer. Chali took up all of my thoughts.

"Find me tonight," she'd said. But, of course, that was impossible. Reaching her at a specific time point with so many centuries between us was like threading a needle with a marble from across the room. But…she'd been so adamant. What if I could? I'd already done the impossible by having a conversation with her. If I had somehow made us visible and audible to each other through a window, who knew what else I could do?

The dig-lab was quiet at night. The recharge lights of the reprogrammed Relion helpers glowed softly against the white, reconstituted walls. I drifted past them in pyjamas, my soft blanket like a cloak. The tech powered up without any trouble. I activated the temporal window, knowing I was foolish to even try.

It was ridiculously easy. The window resolved without any of the usual mental tricks. It was as if the presence of her name in my mind was enough to find her for me.

She looked up from her bedroll in the desert and smiled. All the stars in that wild, untamed sky were hers to command. "I knew you'd come."

"I...I'm glad." The miracle was baffling. *She* was baffling. "But...how?"

She rolled onto her side, leaning into the window, her voice low to avoid waking the rest of her tribe. "You know they're here, don't you? You'll help us get rid of them."

I frowned. "Who?"

'The Helpers. Like this." She drew in the dirt with her finger, a figure taller than human proportions, with a strangely elongated head. My gut filled with ice. Long, egg-shaped heads – hadn't the Relions designed their helper robots in their own image? I accessed my e-lens. The images were blurry but the silhouette was the same.

"The Relions? But...how?" From what little I knew of alien history, the Relions of Chali's time didn't have any kind of transport technology, let alone space travel.

Chali shrugged. A lock of dark hair curled against her throat. "They just appeared. At first, they helped us. They showed us how to build wells and tap into the water beneath the ground. But now they make demands of us. Payment for their help. My people are suffering."

"What kind of payment?" In the dig-lab, there were no stars, no tribe. I was alone in the darkness.

"We give them sacrifices," Chali said. "And we build their symbols. But they say it isn't enough."

She still had the human head I'd seen her with the first day. It'd been dried and threaded with rope from the back of the cranium to a hole in the forehead. "A sacrifice?"

She nodded. Her eyes gleamed. "They take the bodies. They leave us the heads. This was my brother."

She shrugged helplessly and we sat in silence for a long time. I searched for the right words to say, but before I could find them, light flared through the dig-lab, shockingly white and sharp.

Lara blazed in the doorway. "What the hell are you doing?"

I winced at the glare and the temporal window collapsed. "I'm doing my job, Lara. What are you doing?"

"In the middle of the night?" She raised her eyebrows. "Your job is to find something useful for the war, Corin. Not perv at pretty dead girls."

"I'm finding something, trust me." I scowled. "This is big. Technology changing big."

She shook her head. "It better be. You have no idea the kind of pressure the project is coming under right now. The Relions took the Rastek marshal base today. If the galaxy defence system wasn't in place, they'd be here already. They're winning this war and you already spent more than we budgeted shifting the equipment."

"You said I could."

"Yeah." Lara sighed. "Damn, this is a mess. Get some sleep and send me your report tomorrow. You'd better be right."

The next day, military grunts were everywhere. One of them was stationed inside the dig-lab when I got there in the morning. He saluted me, told me I wasn't to use the Relion helper robots any more, then watched everything I did with his enhanced perceptuals and pulse-beams. I had to call Lara to order him out.

"We won't find anything if you distract my people," she snapped. "This takes focus. Unless you know how to run window tech, back the hell off, soldier!"

Chali was waiting for me when the window snapped into place. She was alone in the dunes, lit only by moonlight. She raised her hand towards me and mine reached out to her without conscious thought, hovering above the shimmering plane of the window, almost touching.

Chali took her hand away first. "They're making us shift tomorrow. We're to move to a new location and create the image of a spider."

"I know where that is." My e-lens quickly pulled up its location on a map.

She nodded, her eyes drifting downward. "I think, perhaps, you could meet me there?"

I couldn't keep the smile from my face. "I can try."

"Thank you." She looked up at me, her lips curving upward.

Not knowing how much time we had, I squashed the warmth rising in my chest and got down to business. "Chali, do you know what the Relions are doing there? Why they're making the lines?"

"Relions?" She frowned.

"The Helpers, the ones making you build the lines. We have them in my time, too. We're trying to fight

33

them. It can't be a coincidence."

"It's not." Wind blew Chali's hair loose and she hugged herself. "They speak of you and the war they came from. They say the symbols we make will protect them against the future. I…I think they're scared of you, my love. Of what you can do."

Emotions and thoughts jumbled together. "How?"

She started to shimmer. I struggled to hold the resolution. "They say your windows react with the symbols somehow." She reached towards me again, and for a moment the image snapped into perfect clarity. "I'll try to find out more for when I see you again. Stay safe."

The next day I moved the dig-lab to the spider geoglyph. I bossed the military guys with enough authority that they actually helped with the packing, then, when everything was ready, I gave them the slip. Much easier to ask forgiveness for moving again than permission to spend the funds. I waited the two days it took to set up the new lab and tech before I called Lara and told her everything.

"Corin, what are you doing? What you're telling me is nonsense!" The e-lens transmitted her expression perfectly. "Your military escort are freaking out."

"Wait until they realise what's happening. The Relions are designing the Nazca lines to attack us! We thought we might find weapons in the past – they've gone back there and they're *building* them!"

Lara gave a short sigh. "Where are you, Corin?"

I felt my diaphragm twist. "Why aren't you more excited about this?"

"Because you're not the first person to start

imagining communication with the past. I ran the clip you recorded – I get why you think she was looking at you, but it's just a coincidence. Time-travel technology doesn't exist. We can observe, that's it. Windows, not doorways."

"But Chali says…"

Lara rolled her eyes. "Chali can't say anything! Sound doesn't travel through a temporal window. You know that, Corin. Things are bad enough – do you have to go and have a psychotic break as well?"

I paced the newly constructed lab. My hand lingered over the window tech. None of the recordings had sound. The equipment wasn't set up for it. There was nothing in any of them that would convince Lara of the truth. Hell, listening to her, it was all I could do not to question my own sanity. Replaying it in my mind, though, I knew my connection with Chali was real. "Why did you set the task of finding old weapons if you didn't believe we could do it?"

The e-lens image hovered in place with my pacing. "Nobody believes we can do it, you idiot. I pitched it as a way to keep our funding. For fuck's sake, why would any civilisation just disappear and leave useful weaponry behind?"

"I don't know, Lara. But the Nazca did! They were probably all killed, but they left the lines behind and the fucking Relions are the ones who made the Nazca build them!" I flung the map image of the entire desert up on e-lens for us both to see – pictograms, symbols, temples and lines, all interconnected like some giant robotic circuit-board. "It's something, Lara. They're doing something in the past that's going to hurt us in this war and I need to stop them."

My sight flickered as the e-lens adjusted to incorporate four more portraits, their military green clustered in formation.

"All right, Ms Jenks, we'll take it from here."

Lara pursed her lips tight but said nothing.

"Corin Deer, you are hereby drafted to the Federation military forces. Your RAL scores indicate you'll be a suitable tactical officer. You're to report immediately."

I stopped pacing. "What? No. That's crazy."

"It's not optional, Mr Deer. Failure to report will result in your arrest."

I put the call on hold. My mind was a swirling mess. Obviously, they'd been listening in on my conversation with Lara. They knew what I was working on and they didn't care. Or they didn't believe me any more than Lara did. Either way, if I did what they said, no one would be able to stop the Relions in the past from destroying Chali's people and using the lines device to influence the war in the present. They had to be stopped.

I flicked the call back on in time to hear part of Lara's tirade. "Don't be an idiot, Corin. This isn't just your career anymore. It's your life."

I took a deep breath. "You fight this war your way. I'm going to fight it mine. I'm sorry."

I shut down the connection, killing their protests, then activated the e-lens privacy settings before shutting it off completely. That should slow them down, at least. The first thing they'd do was try to trace me through the e-lens. No e-lens, no trace. As the glow of the newsfeed and data-swamp faded, I felt very alone. I set the perimeter alarms to manual display and activated the window tech.

The window resolved to show Chali in a new dress. The spider symbol was picked out on the fabric. There was a tightness around her eyes that hadn't been there before.

"The lines are nearly finished," she said. "Ours is the only tribe left and they have started to create some kind of hybrid from our children. I'm scared of what they will do to us next."

"Hybrid children?" I swallowed. I was scared too. For Chali and for myself. "Do you know what they're planning to use them for?"

"An attack on the future. That's all I know. That and they're worried because when you visit me, it changes things."

"What things?"

She waved her hands to take in her surroundings. "They worry it will break the symbols so they won't work as intended."

I leaned back against a desk. My mind spun back to the map I'd shown Lara just a short while before. I'd thought then that it looked like a giant circuit board. What if I was right? What if each symbol was a component of circuitry and the lines were connecting wires?

A yellow light on the wall flickered to show that sensors had picked up someone approaching the dig-lab. Lara must have run a trace the second I called her. I had a few minutes more and then I'd have to relocate fast.

"It has to be something to do with temporal

technology," I said. "Otherwise they couldn't expect to attack us in the present. That'd explain why the window tech reacts with the geoglyphs." I stood quickly, my hands flying upward. "Of course! That's why you can see me and we can hear each other! The window is stronger because it's taking power from the Nazca lines weapon!"

Chali leaned closer. "So that means…?"

I grinned at her. "It means I can break their weapon by draining its components. I just have to set up an open temporal window at each site simultaneously."

I started packing equipment as the alarm light flicked to orange. As much spare window tech and reprogrammed Relion robot helpers as I could find, plus any sensor or communication tech that would warn me when the military were getting close.

Chali watched until I was ready to leave. "Will I see you again soon?" she said.

I nodded, using a circuitry welder to fuse the controls on the temporal window. "That should hold it for a while." I paused to smile at her. "We'll have to keep the windows open permanently. We'll be seeing a lot of each other, you and I."

Chali smiled back. "I hope so," she said. "Hurry."

The alarm light turned red and I ran.

That night I hid in the desert and planned. I couldn't run forever. The military men would keep looking and Lara wouldn't do anything to slow them down. I couldn't be sure they would listen to Chali when they found the open window or if she'd still be there when they did. The Relions in her time may have already forced her back to work. It was up to me to save her civilisation and mine from the Relions.

Without my e-lens, I relied on the information in the memory banks of the reprogrammed helper robots I had with me. Fortunately, they had clear maps of the surrounding area and the Nazca lines. I didn't have enough equipment to set up temporal windows at all the geoglyphs, but I knew where to find more.

Lara and her troops wouldn't have enough manpower to do a thorough search of the desert or guard all the sites. They'd cover one or two, while the main force tried to track me by other means. They wouldn't be looking for robots. The geoglyphs' interaction with the temporal window tech seemed to make establishing the windows much easier than before. I was willing to bet I could programme Relion helpers to do it on their own.

"Poetic justice," I muttered as I moved from one robot to the next, "using the Relions' own inventions to destroy their weapon." I sent them out to begin on the first few sites and then settled into the sand to sleep.

I woke a few hours later to a strange glow. Drone hovercopters spiralled darkly overhead. They were not the source of the light and it was too early for dawn.

I risked switching on my e-lens. Immediately I was bombarded with messages and alerts. Lara's code flashed urgent and contained a link to a satellite image of the Nazca desert. There, the source of the strange light was apparent: the geoglyphs were glowing.

I scrambled to the top of the hill and stared over the desert. Sure enough, the lines were shining. Chali's Relions had activated their weapon. My only hope was to get my temporal windows in place before it could take full effect.

"Corin!" Lara's voice broke through via managerial override. "Corin, the military are coming after you and if you don't surrender, they're going to rad-wav the entire desert to stop whatever you've done."

"Damn it, Lara! It's not me – it's the Relions. Destroying the lines *now* will do nothing when they've been activated in the past!"

I ran the satellite recording back over the last two hours. The glowing of the lines was getting brighter. Some kind of powering up sequence. I had time before it got to full strength – I just didn't know how much.

I linked to the robots to check their progress. Several temporal windows were already in place. I messaged a back-up programme. If a robot failed, the remaining robots would see to the rest of the sites.

That left the most difficult site for me: the geoglyph of the humanoid, the site of the dig-team base. I flicked off my e-lens and started the transport.

By the time I reached the base-lab, near blinding white light poured from the lines in the dirt in pulsing waves. If I was going to stop this, it would have to be fast.

Getting inside was tricky, but I knew the base better than the soldiers and I knew Lara's access codes. They trusted the security tech to alert them if I came near but the codes overrode the tech.

The main lab was deserted; the door taped with a military seal. I broke it and slipped inside. I left the lights off and worked in the surreal glow seeping through the windows from the desert outside.

I powered up the temporal window tech only to feel

it shudder, then go still. The lines device was fighting back. Somehow this last window was refusing to connect.

The light outside grew brighter.

I activated the window tech again, and focussed on Chali as hard as I could. I felt the resistance like a sandstorm inside my skull. I gritted my teeth and pushed through it, forcing the tech to pinpoint the time and place I needed. I almost had it – could almost feel it click – when the lab door opened.

"It's over, Corin." Lara and two soldiers stepped into the room. "Whatever you're messing with, just stop. The project is closed down. Everyone's reallocated. Leave it alone and you might get your life back."

The soldiers aimed their pulse-beams at me.

I lifted my hands from the window-tech and held them up in surrender. "If you stop me, the Relions will win."

One of the soldiers began speaking in a monotone as if reading from his e-lens. "Corin Deer, you have been found guilty of desertion in a time of war..."

I closed my eyes to everything else and focussed on Chali. Her whole civilisation would disappear if I couldn't do this. Mine would fall with them if the Relions got the upper hand. The geoglyph outside shone so brightly that I could see the light even through my closed eyelids. It had to be now.

I slammed my hands on the controls and activated the window.

Light flared and a voice shouted. Everything was a blur of colours and then black. There was the sound of weapons fire.

When I could see again, the soldiers were on the ground and Lara was gone.

"You succeeded, my love."

I turned. Chali was behind me. Not a temporal window Chali, but the real, flesh and blood girl. She was here, in the present, with her tribe grouped behind her to fill the lab. "You saved us." She had a gun in her hand. "And I saved you."

I stumbled back a step. "I brought you forward…but how?"

"You made us a time door, my sweet. Our geoglyph tech and your temporal windows combined. It's what we wanted."

My breath was coming in short gasps. "*Your* geoglyph tech?" I flicked on my e-lens and checked the satellite imagery. The giant circuit-board made by the Nazca lines was burned black.

When I switched back, Chali reached out to touch my face. "Of course mine," she said. "Mine and my Helpers."

A scream came from the hallway, and Lara was dragged back into the room. Her arms were gripped roughly by muscular human bodies topped with large, egg-shaped robot heads. My gut knotted. Chali's talk of hybrids had been part truth. Relions weren't aliens; they were cyborgs.

"You've replenished us. We were losing too many against your fighters." Chali gripped my shoulders and turned me toward the window. The external floodlights turned on. I trembled. Only Chali's inhumanly strong hands kept me standing. "And we couldn't have gotten

42

inside your galaxy defence system any other way."

Arrayed across the desert, as far as I could see, were ranks of cyborgs with elongated, egg-shaped heads. An army of Relions.

This one was the result of watching a documentary about the Nazca lines in Peru.   They look like a computer circuit from the air, so I wondered what such a circuit could be designed for, if it was one.   So nothing too deep and meaningful for the inspiration of this one – just a fun little sci-fi disaster story.

SEAHORSES

"So you're a shrink, huh?" George said. He perched on the edge of the plump sofa while Dave took a chair facing. There were too many cushions on that sofa.

"Not exactly. Counselling is a little different to psychiatry."

"Fair enough." George looked him over briefly. Hair too long, glasses, a suit jacket over jeans: awfully young to be telling all your problems to. He glanced away. "You've got a nice office for it."

A small coffee table separated sofa from chairs and an artsy, abstract hibiscus painting hung on the wall. The open window wafted in the smell of the sea and the sound of cicadas. An aquarium filled one corner.

George's first wife had been into aquariums. He remembered their younger hours spent, sunburnt and salty, eating fish and chips in the sand and wading through rock pools along the West Coast with their small son. They'd thrown seaweed at each other and laughed about it, found stranded jellyfish and set them free, and whispered teasing suggestions in each other's ears while brushing fingertips into clinging sea anemones. It had been different back then. You couldn't touch sea anemones in an aquarium.

"What kind of fish have you got?"

"Seahorses. They're one of the few creatures where the father takes care of the young. They're very interesting."

George nodded. "Seahorses." He was a long way from the farm.

"Actually, after our phone conversation, I was hoping to talk to you about fathers."

"Oh?"

Dave leaned forward a fraction. "I was hoping you'd tell me a bit about your dad."

"Oh, um." George frowned. "Well, he's dead."

"Before that?"

George chuckled. "Yeah, I guess that would make a better story, wouldn't it? There's not much to tell, really. He was a good bloke, worked hard and all that. Had a rough life, keeping the farm going and supporting the family, ya know?"

"Sounds like you didn't get to see him much."

"Right. He was a good dad, but. . . he had a lot of responsibilities. I think we would've been mates when I grew up, but there was the heart attack and that was that."

"He worked himself to death before giving you a chance."

George was silent for a long time. "I. . . guess so. Yeah. I mean, he didn't mean to or anything but, yeah, I did miss the chance to get to know him." He shifted in his seat and noticed, for the first time, a box of tissues tucked under one of the chairs. "You get a lot of people crying in here?"

"Sometimes." Dave's gaze was as steady as a fencepost. "I'm interested in how you felt about your dad leaving you like that."

"Well, it meant there was a lot more to do around the place."

"So you got a lot of his responsibility. What did you lose?"

George picked up one of the cushions and ran his fingers along its edge. "I. . ." One of the damned seahorses was hovering right up close to the edge of the aquarium, as if it was trying to press itself through the glass. "Yeah," he said. "Yeah, I lost something. I was twelve when he died. I look at twelve-year-olds now and think that's bloody young to have to be a man. But you know what they say – you just have to move on." He gave a harsh bark of laughter. "There's no point dwelling on stuff, you know?"

Dave leaned forward a little more. "I don't know. Sometimes it helps to spend time talking about stuff. To understand it a bit better."

"Learn from history or else repeat it, you mean?" George grinned. "Worried I'll die young?"

Dave smiled. "Not exactly. I was just thinking. . . my dad left me when I was almost the same age."

"Yeah."

"I was wondering if, maybe, it was similar. I...I missed my dad a lot growing up. I'm lucky that he's still alive to talk to about it now and I wonder, you know, did losing a parent at that same age make it hard to leave?"

For a moment the world was distorted, as though viewed from the inside of an aquarium. His ears filled with the distant sound of the ocean. It took effort to draw air into his lungs. "I. . . yes." He put the cushion down. "It was hard to leave you. It was a difficult situation and I didn't know what to do. I'm sorry."

Dave closed his eyes. "Thanks Dad. I needed to hear that."

They sat silent for a while. Even the cicadas outside the window were gone. George wished he could bring them back.

At last, Dave took a deep breath and stood. "I've got a client coming soon so I need to get my head together. I'm glad you stopped by."

George stood too and gripped his shoulder. "Me too, son." He paused. "Um...maybe we could grab fish and chips and head down to the beach sometime?"

Dave smiled. "I'd like that."

The seahorse turned and glided deeper into the aquarium.

This story is probably one of the more literal inspirations for me. My parents separated when I was young and while Dad and I always loved each other, there was some distance for a long time. Later, when I was training as a counsellor and he became ill, we connected on a much deeper level and built what I believe was a good understanding of each other. Sadly, he passed away before we could make the most of that new phase of our relationship. I miss him greatly.

A Suitor

It is my wedding night and I'm holding a knife stained with blood. My new husband will be disappointed in his expectations. It was inevitable. Only fools believe love can make up for an uneven exchange. I wasn't raised a fool. Yet here I am.

I met Marcus Delanio at the Spring Equinox Ball, a time of heightened power, when innate magic bubbled just beneath the surface of the skin, ready to overwhelm like a fresh sexual awakening. To spill from the unwary and be taken in the heated frenzy of passion.

"There's no such thing as love for the powerful," my mother always warned me. "There are only those who want what you have. If you must give it away, make sure the trade is fair." Her own trade, though it brought her me, had cost her dearly. A point she always remembered until her death, nearly one hundred years ago.

The ballroom was decorated like an artwork, fit for oils and canvas, and brimming with life. Water lilies had been stripped from the canals and woven with wildflowers to festoon the stone pillars from base to vaulted ceiling. A banquet of roast vegetables and meats spread across one end of the great hall, lined with low-powered folk hired as servers.

He approached me, as so many did. He wore a navy frock coat and gold cravat. His dark hair was swept back from his youthful brow and reached to just below his collar and his blue eyes gleamed like polished gems. His smile was just crooked enough to be charming, and bright enough to set any candelabra afire.

"My lady." He bowed slightly, with a touch of awkwardness. Young enough to be my grandchild, he thought he'd charm me into giving up my body and my magic. Young men – particularly pretty ones, all hormones and confidence – are all the same: ever hopeful, sure of their charms. The powerful ones are snapped up before they realise their worth and the lesser gradually fade. But until then, they need to be taken down a peg.

I let my gaze slide past him, taking in the ballroom's marble floor, colourful tapestries hanging from ornately balustraded balconies, and the glittering array of gowns and suits worn by the society present. Many of the guests had stopped to watch the upstart make his move. They'd seen others try their luck before.

"My lady?"

I let my hand rest on the silver bodice of my gown, highlighting the cut of the neckline. "Yes?" I looked no older than he was. Early twenties at best, perky breasts, smooth face, long blond hair threaded with silver ribbons to match the gown clinging to my curves.

It's why they approached me – my appearance and the power it took to maintain it. Power they wanted.

He blushed. "I wondered if you'd like to dance."

I sighed. How original. He would get handsy on the dance floor, perhaps tell me how beautiful my eyes were. Then, if he felt all was going well, he'd suggest we go somewhere more private, relying on his attractiveness and charm to overwhelm my good sense and self-preservation. How did they think I'd lived this long in society? I supposed the strategy worked on partners with less power.

I glanced toward the wide double doors that led out to the courtyard and the canal beyond. "Actually, I believe I'll head out for some fresh air. But my thanks for the offer."

He stepped forward as I turned to walk away. "Might I come with you?" He tilted his head towards a knot of other youths. "I'm an artist and…I find you more interesting than the alternatives."

I hesitated. There was something genuine in his face. He looked suddenly younger and less sure of himself. My gaze strayed to the turquoise handkerchief poking from his jacket pocket like the tip of a leaf emerging in spring and my eyes widened. "You're a courtesan?"

He blushed again and stuffed the coloured fabric back into his pocket. "On a dare," he said. "That isn't why I approached you."

I chuckled. "Of course not." Courtesans specialised in pleasure without joining. There was no sharing of magic in what they did. He could not benefit in it the way most suitors wanted – the equalising of power to his benefit.

A part of me considered taking him with me. For a moment. The simple sensual pleasures of a courtesan would be relaxing and he was an attractive young man. But there were dangers in such things. Should he convince people we had truly lain together and shared our power, the esteem I enjoyed would be forfeit. Not for any puritan reasons, but because the world would believe I had halved my magic with a boy who had little of his own to share. Little difference that my abilities remained the same, the belief would hurt me just as much.

My lips tightened and I shook my head. "I shall take my leave of the evening's festivities. Good night."

My hands clenched the silver fabric of my skirt and I forced myself to move with the graceful glide that was expected of one so powerful. He called after me but I kept moving. It was the last I'd expected to hear from him.

*

The package arrived a few days later as I was preparing Countess Amara Legrande for an art exhibition.

At sixty, the countess was moderately powerful and extraordinarily rich due to a wealthy family and a clever husband. She preferred to make public appearances looking much younger than her true age and made regular use of my favours to achieve this.

"Oooh, something from an admirer?" she clucked as the servants hoisted the large, flat package into the room. It was clearly a painting.

I set down the small tub of poultice I was brushing

across the countess's skin – a watered-down version of the one I used on myself every day as she needed only a fraction of the power I required, being younger to begin with.

I tore the paper from the package. Not the first time I'd been sent a gift from a man trying to woo me for my powers, but this did surprise me. The paper parted to reveal the subject of the painting: me.

I'd never sat for a portrait but the artist had captured my likeness perfectly. The tilt of my cheekbones, the slope of my nose, even the length of my lashes. They were all just right. More than that, the painting had a life to it – a personality. It showed my inner self, shining through, vulnerable and beautiful and strong.

"Oh my," murmured the countess. "That's stunning."

"Mmmm," I said.

There was a note with the painting: "Please come to my exhibit after the opera tonight. You are my inspiration. Marcus."

"Will you go?" asked Amara.

I shrugged and dropped the note on the table. "I doubt it."

The opera that night was beautiful, but it was difficult to concentrate on the music. How could Marcus have painted such a portrait of me after meeting me just once? How much must he have paid attention to me in those few moments? How long had he observed me before hand? Or since?

Could I really be this talented artist's inspiration?

I left before the final encore, scurrying from my box like some socially-inept teen in the throes of her first crush. The note was in my purse. The thought of it made my face hot.

Outside, the cool air and familiar scent of the canals was soothing. I crossed the cobblestones of the courtyard, leaving the music and light of the opera house behind, replacing brass and strings with gentle lapping of water against stone and the calls of evening gondoliers.

I waved aside a footman who offered me a vessel and crossed the bridge on foot. The time to myself under the stars was restful.

I let my feet take me where they willed, trailing my fingers long the stonework of the old city. Moonlight sparkled on the water of the canals as I wandered along their edges. The spell of the summer night kept me moving until at last it was broken by an increase in other traffic, both by foot and canal. I had made my way to the art gallery and Marcus's exhibition.

Patrons flooded into the building like colourful birds flocking to discarded bread but I held back, undecided.

What did it mean that he'd invited me in such a way? Would the exhibition contain other portraits of me? What if that was all there was? Did Marcus have feelings for me? Or was this all simply another seduction ploy?

"You came." Marcus spoke quietly. I'd been so lost in my thoughts, I hadn't noticed his approach. "The exhibit is inside."

I kept my gaze on the water of the canal. "Perhaps I'm just out for a walk."

"It's a dangerous part of town for it," he said. "They say a girl was killed under that bridge a few nights ago.

Blood magic practitioners."

I sighed. "How old?"

"They didn't say. Young, I think."

I nodded. "Of course. The sacrifice must be a virgin. But people have forgotten that the age is important. Bleeding some hapless teen to death is virtually worthless."

"Really?" I caught his surprised expression out of the corner of my eye.

"It was more common when I was younger." My mother had dabbled and even then, she'd been one of the few who still knew the ways of it. Her ability made her life bearable with only half the magic she was born with. Now all anyone remembered was the sacrifice, and not how to best make use of it.

"Right." He shifted uncomfortably, suddenly reminded of my age. "Of course, no one weak enough to need blood magic could be any threat to you."

I chuckled. "How do you know *I'm* not using blood magic?"

He snorted. "Please. My mother says she remembers you from when she was a child and you looked just as you do today. You'd have to slaughter forty virgins a day to stay looking like you do with blood magic." He tilted his head to the side and wrinkled his nose at me. "I think someone would have noticed."

I laughed. "Yes, perhaps they would have."

The light from the street lamps played on the water. Then he said, softly. "Did you like the painting?"

I turned to face him. "It was an intriguing gift."

He leaned on the railing and smiled that slightly crooked smile. "You're an intriguing subject."

"You've seen more of me than I expected."

His cheeks coloured. "I notice beauty," he said. "The curse of the artist."

"I notice flattery," I said. "It's the curse of age. Although you've gotten better at it."

His cheeks flushed deeper in the moonlight. "It's not flattery when it's true. I've always noticed you. And loved you."

My eyes narrowed. "Talk of love is dangerous to one of power. It almost always hides a desire to take what we have."

"But many people do join for love and give up the desire for more magic," he said. "Not all of us are consumed by it."

"True." I shrugged. "My mother did. She was very powerful and my father had hardly any magic at all. She spent the rest of her life missing her power. I can't afford to do the same. My power is how I support myself. I'm alone in this world. I must rely on myself."

He touched my arm. "You can rely on me."

I raised an eyebrow. "Really?"

He nodded, his face full of puppy-dog seriousness. "I would marry you if I could."

I snorted. "I'm sure you would. And in the consummation, claim half of my power while giving me half of your much smaller portion in return."

He shook his head. "I don't want your power. I want you."

"Well, one doesn't come without the other, does it?"

"What if it could?"

I frowned. Was he even serious? "What do you mean?"

"What if I could bring a similar amount of power to the joining?"

"How?"

"I'll find a way." He stared out into the canal. A gondolier pushed his small craft past us in long, slow strokes. Finally, Marcus said, "Who would you say is your nearest rival for magic?"

Laughter bubbled up inside me. This was how he intended to even the match? By taking from others to bring to me? "The Grand Duke," I said. "But even if he fancied young men, he will be just as cautious about who he lays with as I am. You'll get the same answer from him."

Marcus pushed his hair back from his eyes, letting them bore earnestly into mine. "The journey may take many steps but the destination is you."

I smiled. "Perhaps."

A few weeks later, Countess Amara Legrande was crying in my salon. "I can't believe I was so foolish," she sobbed. "But he's a handsome young artist and he flattered me so. I wanted to believe him."

I touched her arm. "Amara, I'm so sorry. Does your husband know?"

The countess shook her head. "Not yet. But I now have much less magic than I did before. The next time my husband and I…" She broke off.

"Your magic will be equalised and he will lose a chunk of his magic as a result. He will realise what you've done. Amara, you must tell him before that happens."

She nodded, wiping her eyes. "I know," she said. "But please, don't tell anyone else. If it became public knowledge, I don't know what we'd do."

"Of course."

A painting of the countess arrived the next day.

Two more paintings were delivered the following month. They showed women more magically powerful than the countess. A month after that, another, even more gifted.

I met with him after that. "You should stop," I said. "You're taking people's magic – ruining their lives."

"I can't." He took my hands in his. "Don't you see? If losing some of their magic ruins their lives, then they were relying on it too much in the first place. I have to gain enough power to be worthy of you and this is the only way I can do it."

As the months stretched on and every few weeks brought another painting, another conquest bringing him another portion of magic to make himself more palatable to the next, I wondered: was he truly doing this to win me? Or would I simply be the end game? His final conquest to achieve maximum power?

As his power grew, he became flashy, using it at public gatherings. His art gallery became known for exotic displays of magically-enhanced plant growth and lights, highlighting the paintings for sale. Women and men flocked around him, his evident magic and good looks making him not merely palatable but a desired match among the powerful. Few of those he'd been with were brave enough to speak of their dalliances with him for fear of revealing they had lost power.

At last, Marcus brought me the last painting – that of the Grand Duke himself. "I've done it," he said. "I've gained all the magic I can to be with you." His eyes filled with tears. "Please, you must believe that I care nothing for any of it. I want only for us to be together."

And I, the fool for love my mother warned me about, agreed.

We lay together as husband and wife. When it was done, he held me close and whispered into my ear. "Tomorrow, we will wake together as equals."

He is in my bed still, as I hold the knife. I open the window and throw it into the canal. I will need it no more. The pot of youth-giving poultice follows the blade and sinks beneath the water. The virgin blood in the mix is useless now. I am no longer a virgin.

I close my eyes and picture my mother teaching me the ways of blood magic. "Virgin blood," she would say. "Living or dead. The older the better. You'll be your own best supply."

My magic was never more than pitiful, having taken after my father, but my virginal blood …the power of that had grown with the years. At first, barely enough to do little spells, then enough to keep age at bay. Then larger feats, youth and immortality, if I was dosed with it every day.

I push up the sleeves of my night dress and stare at the scars. No more would I bleed myself every day. Marcus has brought me his power.

Tomorrow we will wake as equals.

In this story, I wanted to explore the added meaning human society gives to sex. Throughout history, virginity and sexual connection has been loaded with meaning and consequence – that it was a giving of yourself in a way that is more than physical. I wanted to bring this into a magical realm and see what that was like. What if the giving was of magical power and virginity and sex had different consequences for that magic? This was the result of that pondering.

SPRING

His languid hand drew swirls like koru on her belly, warm beneath his fingers and not yet showing the roundness to come. The sun dabbed light across the sheets, green like new buds in Spring, fertile. She smiled and he moved his touch upward across her breasts. "Don't squeeze them," she warned. "They're tender at the moment." He grabbed them anyway and she squealed with laughter. "Get off, ya jerk."

He nuzzled her neck, then pulled away, dragging the sheet back even as she tried to clutch it close. "Such language in front of the baby. Shocking!" He leaned to kiss her stomach then swung his legs over the edge of the mattress. "Time to get up anyway."

Underpants in the second drawer, trousers in the wardrobe. A shirt. Then, somewhere between buttoning the shirt and buckling the belt, the world shifted.

"Oh!" When he turned her eyes were wide and when she held up her hand there was red on it. "I think we need to call the midwife. Now."

He wasn't even close to ready. He hadn't learned

the route to the hospital, rehearsed it, or packed a bag. Why would he? That sort of thing was months away. He shouldn't have needed to know where to go, yet somehow he found the way.

The hospital sprawled large and smug in its hardened bed of asphalt, feeding on the desperation of swallowed souls. Intestinal corridors squeezed them through, swift and faceless, until, at last, he watched her belly smeared with gel beneath an ultrasound scanner.

It moved and pressed, methodical in its purpose. In the darkened room, the light from the screen shifted like water, then held frozen, a sculpture in ice and static. Click marked a measure point, then, click, another. The operator typed a code, re-angled the scanner, and rolled a dial on the panel of the machine. He didn't know what that meant.

The scanner moved again, an oddly-shaped snail sliming a path of gel across her skin.

"Is it true what they say? Is that stuff cold?"

She nodded, her eyes meeting his for a moment, then turned to search the ceiling. "Yeah, it's cold."

"Some pregnancies get bleeding and it isn't always bad," the operator said. The machine hummed softly, determined to be ambiguous. "We'll do an internal scan as well, just to be thorough." The snail retreated, replaced by a wand.

He looked at her. "Are you okay with that?"

She nodded, her face tight, and closed her eyes. The machine hummed on, the screen shifted, froze, and clicked. Her body was invaded while he held her hand. "It'll be worth all this to know it's okay."

The operator touched her shoulder. "We're all done.

I'll be back in a moment."

She pulled a curtain across the door as she left, shielding them from sight, but not from sound or smell. The hospital's bowels rumbled with trundler beds and nurses' chatter and its antibacterial stench wafted thickly over them both.

The hand in his squeezed tightly. He squeezed back, guarding her from harm with impotent strength. "I don't know how she can see anything on that screen."

That got a faint smile.

Then the operator was back with a man in a sterile white coat. "There's no heartbeat," he said. "I'm sorry. Your baby can't live without a heart."

He wondered at that, blankly, his wife's soft sobs warring against the machine's hum.

A person cannot live without a heart. Why not? Doctors do. How else could they say such things? The world should have stopped – everywhere – just for a moment. But in this place, instead, it bustled on. Without a heart.

"It's like removing a Band-aid," the white coat said. "You can wait for it to slowly peel away on its own – and eventually it will – or you can pull it off quick and it's over all at once."

She wiped her eyes. "All at once." she said. He agreed.

So there was a gown and a hair net and shoes made of paper. A nurse spoke with them briefly before the needle came. "No sex for a couple of weeks after."

He touched her shoulder. "At least your breasts will be less tender by then." Less full, round, and changing.

There was nothing for anyone to say until the

anaesthetist came. "You'll have to stay in the waiting room until she's ready to go home."

The waiting room was numb; a purgatory of nothing. He took one breath each time it was due and waited. He stared at the wooden frame on the wall and never saw the print it held. His watch told tales of things gone wrong, but the room did not permit time. He had left her with strangers. There were no friends in this place.

At last, the nurse returned in her white smock halo. "We can bend the rules now and then, you know. Come and see her for a moment. She's just waking up." Afterward, he felt he should have been able to remember the face of someone so kind, but his eyes were only for her.

"How are you feeling?"

Her eyelids dragged open a little. "Hi," she whispered. Her body was wholly her own now, no more than that. "I'm sorry."

He touched her hand, mindful of the drip penetrating her skin, and bit back worthless platitudes. "Me too."

"She still needs to rest," the nurse said softly. "Take a walk outside. We'll call you when she's ready to go home."

Those digesting in the waiting room looked up as he passed but he could not stop.

He hurried through the corridors, dodging wheelchairs and grief until he was spat out into concrete, chilled sunlight and shiny cars discarded in endless rows.

The glass double doors slid open and shut behind him. Other souls pushed past and were swallowed. He stared out into a world slowed and shifted. Dead leaves traced koru in the wind. Spring was a long way off.

"Spring" is another example of me processing my real life emotions through fiction. My wife and I experienced six miscarriages in our quest for children. A quest that we ultimately moved away from to develop our lives in other ways. The last one was in the second trimester and the song, "Big Girls Don't Cry" by Fergie was playing every time I left the hospital room throughout those two horrible days. It grew to have a strong significance for me.

Miscarriage is something that is rarely talked about and can have significant impact on both parents - often in different ways. Writing about this fictional couple was cathartic and helped me feel better as well as raising awareness of the issue.

This story was printed in the Northern Advocate after winning third prize in their short story competition.

It is the only one of my stories that my wife has chosen never to read because of the painful content.

CUT AND COLOUR

This one had a certain shaggy quality to him. A kind of out-of-control Beatles' mop. It was like a blank canvas. A fresh page. A newly-tilled garden.

A new client always made me smile.

He plucked at his jacket and chewed his lip. Nervous, as if he hadn't been in a place like this before. He probably hadn't. He looked like a Cheap Cuts at the mall kind of guy. But something had brought him here, to the most prestigious salon around. Something had brought him to me.

I put on my bright, welcoming face. "Hey there, Sunshine. What can we do for you today?"

He stepped up to the counter. "I have an appointment. My name is Dave Mackleby."

"Of course you do, come on through. May I take your jacket?"

He shrugged out of it and I hung it up for him. It was more expensive than his other clothes – jeans and a t-shirt. This was a new blazer. He'd been shopping recently. New success then. Even better.

"So what do you do, Dave?"

He took a deep breath. "I'm an author. Actually, my novel just hit the bestseller list."

"Really?" I led him to the washbasin and sat him down. "That's wonderful! Congratulations." That explained the new money, clothes and hair stylist.

He smiled as he leaned back and I began to wash his hair. "Thanks. Actually, that's why I'm here. My publisher wants me to do a book tour and apparently I need a certain image for publicity."

I put reassurance into my voice as I stroked the shampoo through his hair. Warm, relaxing water ran through my fingers and I massaged his scalp. "You've come to the right place. That's exactly what we do here. You'll look every bit the stylish literary genius by the time I'm done today."

He relaxed under my touch. They always do.

"She's not wrong," one of the other clients called out. "Del is the best there is."

"Thanks Liz." Elizabeth Cornell was a golfing legend. She came in to have her roots coloured and her hair cut every six weeks like clockwork, unless she was overseas for a tournament. I used to do her myself, but lately I'd had Meredith take over. "How's my girl treating you over there?"

Meredith stayed silent, painting colour into foils.

"She's great," Liz said. "Almost as good as you."

I chuckled. "Flatterer. You know our rule – only the best for the best. Meredith is excellent." I added conditioner to Dave's hair and massaged it in. "Liz here is a pro golfer. How's the golfing world going these days, Liz?"

Dave made an interested noise but kept his eyes closed against the spray.

Liz wrinkled her nose. "Could be better. I seem to have lost my mojo lately."

Understatement of the year. She hadn't placed in a golf tournament in thirteen months. That's the reason Liz was now one of Meredith's clients. Call me horrible, but once they lose their mojo, I lose interest. Some people say my clients are the rich and famous. In reality, they're the talented, skilled, and successful.

"Well, you just have to work at it," I said sweetly. "The only way to success is hard work. Isn't that right, Dave?"

Dave sat up a little so I could towel dry his hair. "God yes. You wouldn't believe how long I've been writing to get good enough for the success I have now. And people say it happened overnight. That's one bloody long night, if you ask me!"

Meredith dipped her brush back into the little pot of colour she'd mixed. "Look at Del," she said. "When she started here she could barely use scissors. Now she owns the place and people can't get in without a recommendation from an existing client."

I struggled to keep the scowl from my face. Some people's memories were far too long.

"I had a good teacher. I learned a lot from the previous owner before she... lost her passion for the work." I pulled the towel from Dave's head and gestured to him to follow me to one of the cutting chairs. "Now then, what ideas do you have for how you'd like your hair to look?"

An hour later, I sent Dave on his way. He had a huge smile on his face and kept checking out his reflection as he made his way to the door. I'd given him shorter sides with longer on top and shown him several different ways to style it. He looked modern and intelligent – especially when matched with a pair of intellectual glasses. I even managed to sell him three types of product and recommended a photographer for his publicity shots.

Meredith had long since finished with Liz Cornell and I sent her home for the day, locking the door behind her.

I looked over the salon. My salon. Marble floors, ornately framed mirrors, soft coloured walls, and classical music. I flicked off the music and picked up a broom. Bestselling author, Dave Mackleby's hair was still on the floor around the chair.

I swept it up carefully, making sure to get every loose clipping into a neat and tidy little pile. He had such lovely soft, chestnut-coloured hair. I scooped it into a container from behind the reception desk and carried it out the back, past the storeroom with its bottles of colours and freshly laundered towels, to my office.

Nobody else ever came into this room. Not since I took over the salon.

The walls were lined with newspaper clippings and trophies – the newest ones to the front, older ones to the back. "Surprise newcomer beats club record," declared one clipping. That belonged to the golden golf trophy on the nearest shelf. I remembered the surprised looks on their faces when I'd won it – an amateur entrant completing all 18 holes in fewer strokes than any professional.

Next to that was the bravery medal I'd received from the mayor for carrying an unconscious man from a burning building. "I'm stronger than I look," I'd told the press. "And you know what they say about adrenaline."

Further back were the hairdressing awards. I'd won those quickly enough once I had what I needed from the salon's previous owner.

I placed the container of Dave's hair on my desk and sat in the chair.

Clients with strengths and talents and skills. Oh, how I loved them.

I hoped Dave enjoyed his book tour. He would have those memories to lean on when he discovered the muse had left him and times got hard.

I leaned forward, over the container, closed my eyes and breathed deep. The smell of it – shampoo, natural oils, damp hair…inspiration, imagination, literary skill. I soaked it in. I could feel the essence of his gifts leaching from the hair like a cheap, washable dye. My body quivered and I licked my lips, tasting his hair on my tongue. Tasting his talent.

I opened my eyes. The hair in the bowl was now grey and brittle.

I smiled and pushed it aside, picking up a pad and pen instead. I'd always wanted to write a bestseller. I reached for my new talent – Dave's strength, now mine - and began to write.

"The Cruel Cut. A novel by Delilah Samson."

This idea came while listening to the radio and a song with the name Delilah played. My wife and I both looked at each other and said "What if the Biblical Delilah was a hairdresser?"

Delilah in the Bible, of course, was the woman who took Samson's strength by cutting his hair. In this story, I wanted to make her something more – here she can steal any strength, any talent, from a person by cutting their hair. It ties into a fear I often have when starting a new writing project – what if I've lost the ability to write? This story was a fun way to bring the two together.

THE APPLE TREE

The funeral smells like apple blossoms. Sarah had loved her apple tree – was obsessed by it, really. I can almost hear her explaining it again. "They bud, grow, then fall. It's life and death, all contained."

Beneath the blossoms is the musty scent of old wood. The church pews have long since lost the gloss of varnish, but shine from the polishing of a thousand shifting parishioners in their Sunday best. High above our heads, at regular intervals along the walls, the orange bars of the heaters burn with holy passion, leading the eye to the front of the church. There, the bronze figure of Christ gazes down from the cross at Sarah's coffin, dark with floral highlights on silver handles.

I wish I could turn away but I'm captured by those bronze, staring eyes. If there's a Heaven, Sarah will be in it and I pray that Christ doesn't tell her what I've done.

*

The first time I saw Sarah Fairway, I was tagging her fence. She was a shadow in the porch-light and a voice calling, "Who's out there?" I kept my finger on the spray-can nozzle until a male voice shouted, "Hey!" Then I ran, disappearing into the local park.

Stu and I laughed about it afterward. Laughed at how long it'd taken her to paint out our tags the last time and how much bigger we'd made them now.

"Oh man," Stu said. "White fuckin' pickets!"

"Begging for it."

"You know what we should do?" Stu said. "The library roof. They just painted it."

I thought about it. It was 9.45 and I hadn't had dinner. "Tomorrow. I'm starved."

The house was quiet when I got home. Dad scowled at the TV from a sea of empty bottles.

"Fuck you're useless, boy. You think you can swan in whenever you like?"

"I'll deal with him, Barry. Don't worry," Mum placated. The bruise of the week was on her cheekbone, dark in the centre and yellow at the edge.

Dad snorted and picked up the tail of a cigarette from an old jar lid. "Yeah, you deal with him. Don't forget to wipe his ass while you're at it."

9:45 was too soon to go home.

*

My mother sits across the church from me. She's perched on the edge of the pew like a frail, frightened bird, her dark, feathered hair aglow from the heaters. My father is nowhere to be seen, but I've long since given up hoping that means he's gone. Mum's makeup is very thick.

I frown. I'm not sure she ever met Sarah.

Someone clears his throat next to me and I look up

to see the undertaker. "Excuse me, you're one of the pallbearers, right?"

I try not to recoil. "No."

He looks puzzled. "I thought…"

"I…no. They asked me to, but…I can't."

"Okay." He nods, knowingly. "That's all right. I'll sort it out."

*

The next time I saw Sarah, I was painting over the tags on her fence as part of probation. Everywhere else I had to repaint, the people had stayed hidden behind twitching curtains, once shouting insults that I rebuffed with a lifted finger.

Sarah waited until the sun was at its hottest, then walked boldly across the lawn with a tray of glasses and juice.

She was maybe in her fifties. Her hair was streaked with grey but she didn't hide it or dye it. She wore it long and loose, a sensual, feminine tangle around her face and shoulders. Her dress flowed in waves to her bare feet. Her fingers were splotched with dabs of paint, bright along the back and huddled darkly under the nails.

Stu glanced at me from under his cap. I raised my eyebrows back at him.

"Would you gentlemen like to take a break?" Her voice had a trace of an accent.

I shrugged and put the paintbrush down. White paint smeared the grass. Sarah handed me a glass and I drank it – real juice, not cordial. Stu took his but just held it. I wondered if she'd put something in it for revenge, but then she took a sip of her own.

She stepped past us to look at the fence. The tags

still showed through the first layer of paint. "I've been wondering what they mean," she said, and paused.

Stu and I kept silent.

She gestured toward the fence. "The symbols - tags. Can you tell me what they represent?"

She stood there, her bare feet next to my paintbrush, and waited for my answer.

It would be ridiculous to tell her. How could someone like her understand? Understand that the t in Stu's tag was raised like a cross for his brother who crashed on the way home from church? Or that the slope on the n in mine was the exact shape of my baby's sleeping outline the first and only time I ever saw her?

I looked at Stu. "Nothing," he said. "They're just tags."

Sarah nodded. "And yours?"

I opened my mouth to give the same answer, but instead said, "Family stuff."

"Okay." She nodded again, her crow's feet crinkling a little. "And the colour?"

"It's red."

Her cheek twitched. "Yes, I see it's red. Why red? What does it mean?"

Behind me, Stu gave a snort of laughter, but I answered anyway. "I dunno. Kinda like it's a strong colour. Like, making it known I'm here."

"Possessive?" She quirked an eyebrow.

"I guess." I tugged at my hoodie. Damn, she was nosey. I searched for the paint brush. "I dunno. Maybe."

"Good." Her voice was barely above a whisper. She nodded slowly then spoke with more volume.

"Good. Well, enjoy your drinks, boys. I don't want to keep you from your work. Perhaps you could bring the glasses in for me when you're done?"

When she was gone, Stu elbowed me in the shoulder. "Someone's got the hots for you, bro!"

"Shut up."

"Serious, man." He wagged his eyebrows at me. "You should report it." He put on a high-pitched whiney voice. "Please miss, that lady molested me and now I can't work or nuffink." He laughed loudly.

I picked up my paint brush. "Whatever, man. Let's just get this done and get out of here."

*

The photograph on the casket doesn't do her justice. She still looks the way I remember – six years haven't aged her much – but it doesn't show her essence. She could have captured it herself in a painting, but this is only the work of a camera.

I turn my attention back to the minister as he extols the virtues of a good life. I'm not sure Sarah was religious. I'm not sure he knew her at all. The congregation is a strange mixture of small town provincials and art world glitterati. I realise I only knew a small part of her.

We stand and sing a hymn. We sit and the minister drones on. His suit is black, cheap and uninspired. His funeral suit, I imagine. He probably has a different one for weddings – navy blue, perhaps, with a brighter tie. Sarah would have critiqued the use of colour. So many shades left unexplored. There is a reading, and then the minister speaks again: "I invite anyone who would like to come up and say a few words about their relationship with Sarah Fairway to do so now."

I sit very still. Before anyone else can move, a familiar figure stands at the front of the church. He must have told people he was family to get that close. I suppose in a way he was.

Julian's iron hair is gelled to perfection, his clothing immaculate. He has a tiny sprig of apple blossom on his lapel and has somehow managed to match the colour with his belt. He steps up to the podium with an air of cultivated campness.

"When Sarah was first diagnosed, I was one of the few people she told. She didn't know how much time she had left and, for some strange reason, decided to spend it in this small town. I couldn't understand it!" He beams a winning smile at the crowd amidst a scattering of titters.

"But eventually I did. She wanted time away from the city to paint. To leave a body of work that would be a legacy." His eyes find me out and I look away. I set my jaw and feel my stomach tighten. "The apple tree works are her genius, her study of transience and mortality. The study didn't end the way she hoped, but the work is brilliant. Even if she'd done nothing else, she'll be remembered for that.

"Sarah was not only a great visionary in the art of painting, but also in finding the beauty in people. She was responsible for fostering the talent of a local young man who has become something of a celebrity in the art world." This time there is no escaping his gaze. I force my face into a gratified smile. How many of these people remember the me from back then?

The room is too warm. I wish I could take off my

jacket. I turn the programme over and over in my hands. There's a small note on the back: "An exhibition including Sarah's work will be in the Pohutukawa Room until the end of the week." When it comes to promotion, Julian can't help himself.

Someone taps my shoulder. "He wants you to go up and say something."

Julian's voice is golden syrup, sweet with just enough dark for a funeral. "For those of you who don't know, this is Aiden Maukei, Sarah's protégé and one of the best artists I know."

I stand up.

*

"Sarah, what are you doing? The kid's a vandal – he could be dangerous!" Julian's voice reached me from the next room. He was the classic faggot, complete with just a hint of lisp.

"Julian," Sarah sounded reproachful. "He has something. I'd like to explore it."

"Oh please. How much talent can he have? And what about your work? I don't think you should be taking risks with your time now."

There was a clatter, like a cup being set down too hard. "I'll do what I like with my time, thank you very much. You don't have the right to-" Then her voice was too low to hear. Strange people, these. They got quieter when they argued. Weird.

The inside of Sarah's house was a clash between my Nan's lounge and a kindergarten crafts area. The floral pattern on the drapes was all pastel vines on a background the same cream as the couch. There were splotches of paint on the couch arms that Nan would have had a fit about, and empty tubes on the carpet around an easel. The drapes were pulled back exposing the apple tree in the yard. Beside the easel was a small table covered with brushes and more paints.

I flipped through the canvases stacked against the wall. Some were empty, most brimmed with colour and half formed shapes – the tree outside and the apples. They were certainly better than what I'd attempted so far. I paused at one of the paintings – a half rotted apple in purple and blue on shocking pink grass. Weird.

Sarah bustled in.   "I'm sorry about that, Aiden. Where were we?"

I shrugged.   "We can flag it if your boyfriend's upset."

"Actually, he's my agent."   She gave me a wicked grin.   "But I think you know he's not my boyfriend."

I laughed.   "Yeah, I figured."

"Okay, so then back to work."   She lifted the apple she wanted us to paint and held it out to me.   "What colour is this?"

"Red."

"Anyone can see that.   What else is it?"

"Green.   And…" I looked closer.   "Yellow?   And kinda orange just there."

"Good.   What else?"

"I don't know."

"Do you see the different shades of red?"

"Ye-ah."   I did, now.

"And the spots of light?"

"Yeah, there's almost white – but it's not really white.   Kind of grey.   And…" I frowned.   "Black?"

Sarah nodded.   "Good.   You're starting to see what

your eyes show you, not what your brain thinks you're seeing. Most people will paint the apple red or green, and they're wrong. You're learning to paint the colours that are really there so that your painting shows reality. It'll be better for it."

I poked at the array of brushes on the table. "Your paintings don't always have the right colours," I said.

She smiled. "Once you master the true colours, you can change them to add meaning. I can add indigo and purple, and give the apple a kind of glow in a darkened surrounding and it becomes a symbol of life and desire in a world of darkness, hope for the denizens of the night." Her smile widened into a grin. "Or something like that. Do you see? There's purpose behind it. Once you can see the possibilities, you can make a choice."

*

The ceremony is over. The coffin makes its way down the aisle and out the door, trailing mourners like autumn leaves in the wind. I join them, but a touch on my arm makes me stop. Stu's tobacco-stained fingers pull away as I turn.

"Well, fuck me," he says. "It *is* you. Wasn't sure you'd be here, mate." He pushes the sleeves of his hoodie up to reveal rough tattoos across his fingers and forearms. He hadn't had those when I'd seen him last. His eyes rove over my black designer suit, bright shirt and shiny dress shoes. "That your boyfriend up there, before, was it?"

I give him my polite smile. "Good to see you Stu. I wasn't sure you'd be here either."

He shrugs and leans against the back of a pew. "Nothing much else to do around here."

Julian appears from nowhere. "Aiden, I want to introduce you to the gallery manager..."

The publicity rounds are endless with Julian. I nod. "Julian, this is Stu. We used to hang out back before I met Sarah."

Stu slouches, avoiding Julian's proffered hand. "Yeah, well. Haven't seen each other for ages. Not since Mr Great Artist got the scholarship and buggered off to the city." He nods his head in the direction of the casket. "She arranged that for you, I heard."

I sigh. She'd put in my application and vouched for me, criminal record and all. "Yeah."

*

My knuckles hurt when I knocked on Sarah's door. They left a smudge of blood on the white wood. My face hurt, too. My lip was thick and my cheek puffy.

The door opened and Sarah's eyes widened. "Aiden! What happened?"

"I..." I licked my lip and blinked back tears. I tried again but my voice still cracked. "My dad got drunk and..." I shrugged and looked away.

"Paint it."

"What?" My lip hurt when I spoke. My tongue poked at the split and tasted the damage.

"*Paint it!*" She grasped my wrist and pulled me into the studio. She was stronger than I expected. A demoness. She thrust my bloody hand onto the pristine canvas. The colour of the fight smeared livid.

"Red," she said, letting go of my hand and reaching for the tubes of oils to squeeze onto the palette. "The colour of anger, pain, passion, blood. Paint it! Paint!"

I reached for the paint. After that, time was a blur.

Sarah disappeared. The world disappeared. There was only me and the canvas and the colours of my emotions. I worked with brushes, but often just with my hands, the cut knuckles stinging with pigment. I worked with sobs, with screams of rage, with impotent frustration and furious change. The canvas soaked it all in, and the paint gave it form.

When I was done, I sank slowly into a chair, exhausted. The painting was abstract, raw, and personal. I let my stained hands rest on my jeans and stared.

"See?" Sarah's voice was barely audible but it was enough for me to remember there was someone else in the room.

I glanced over my shoulder. Julian was there too. He peered past me at the painting and his tongue flicked over his bottom lip. "Fuck," he said, with no hint of his usual effeminate accent. "I take it all back."

Sarah smiled and put her hand on my shoulder. "What did I tell you? The boy has talent."

Later, she made us all coffee and we drank it, sitting together, staring at my work while the warm liquid loosened my anxiety. "It…it's good, isn't it?"

Sarah smiled and nodded slowly. "It's very good. I knew it would be. It's the curse of the artist – all our best work comes from pain."

I took another sip, frowning. "What about your apple tree stuff? Everyone says that's some of your best work. It…doesn't seem painful."

"Life and death isn't painful?" Her smile faded a little - still a smile, but somehow sad. "Look at the base of the apple tree. There's a plaque there for my husband and son." She looked away. "We were out celebrating one night. I'd won an award. I didn't think I'd drunk very much but…perhaps I had." She turned back with a shrug. "Their ashes are under the tree. It reminds me to hope – to remember that all things die but life comes around again. Even for apples."

"Oh." I nodded slowly. "It's the curve in your tag."

She smiled for real this time. "I suppose it is."

*

I offer Stu a ride to the graveside.

"Nah," he says. "Not really into that. See you at the house though. Free food."

It's a small graveyard on a hill. There are older, moss-edged gravestones on the far side; newer, shiny stones on this side; and cheaper, low to the ground markers near the the fence. Pine trees grow on the other side of the fence. No apples here.

They lower Sarah's coffin into the ground and I turn away as others say their goodbyes. As I walk back to the car, Julian joins me.

"Aiden, I need to have a few minutes with you privately when we get to the house. Sarah left something for you. She wanted me to give it to you today."

*

It was dark when the painting lesson finished. Sarah turned the porch light on for me as I left but it didn't quite reach the street. The familiar hiss of a spray can sounded loud in the dark.

"Hey! What are you doing?"

Stu pulled back his hoodie and glared at me. "What the fuck does it look like?" He turned back and continued his tag on Sarah's fence.

"Don't." I made a grab for the can but Stu pulled away.

"What the fuck, man? White pickets, remember? This is what we do. Or we did when we were mates. Before you went all gay on me with this art shit." He held up the spray can and shook it. The mixer ball rattled inside. "This is our art, man. You need to fuckin' choose who your mates are."

My chest tightened. "Come on. You know we're mates. The art stuff doesn't change that."

"Well, you better find a way to prove it, 'cause your mates don't know you any more. Who matters to you more? Me or her? You gotta make a choice." Stu turned and walked away. My one true friend, walking away because I couldn't prove my loyalty.

I looked at the house, quiet and still, then at Stu's back. "Wait," I hissed. "Wait!"

"What?"

"Don't do the fence." I took a deep breath. "If you want it to mean anything, do the tree."

"Show me," he said.

The light from the porch threw shadows to make shapes in the branches. I couldn't see any apples, only creatures I didn't understand. The bark was too rough to hold the tag shape well, but I could fix that.

"You got your knife, Stu?" He always carried a carving knife he'd lifted from a camping store. It was good for etching. He handed it over wordlessly.

I cut into the bark, slicing it away from the smooth wood underneath. It was difficult going, but the knife was sharp enough. We would need a large space of clear wood. A large canvas on which to make our marks.

Wood chips fell around me, sap oozed. I cut my thumb but barely noticed. Slowly, I worked my way around the tree, widening the clear wood. At last, I met the place where I'd started. Our barkless canvas wrapped around the tree, two hands high and ready.

"You do that side and I'll do this one," I said. "Just like always."

I held the knife out to him, but he took a step back and spread his hands wide. "I'm not signing that, mate."

"What? Why?"

"You've fucking ring-barked it. That whole tree's gonna die."

*

The studio is awash with people. The benches have been cleared of paints and canvas and covered instead with food – sausage rolls fight for space with canapés. The noise is overwhelming. My hand is grasped and my shoulder squeezed many times as Julian leads me through the crowd.

"Lovely eulogy, Aiden."

"She'll be missed."

Julian pulls open the door to what was Sarah's bedroom and we step inside. It's quiet. The room has a different floral design to the lounge, the colours muted and soft. Lace edges the pillows on the bed. Propped against the wall, is a large canvas, wrapped in brown paper.

Julian lifts the package onto the bed. "She wanted you to have this."

*

The last time I saw Sarah Fairway, she was sitting at the base of her dying apple tree. Her hand never left it, fingers tracing the edge of the bark and across the gash. Her eyes were the colour of pain. I sat beside her and did my best to meet them.

"Can the tree guy do anything?"

Sarah shook her head. "It won't recover. There's too much damage. The best thing to do now is to cut it down before it rots and gets dangerous."

"Oh." I looked away. The plaque for her husband and son glinted in the sunlight. "Maybe you could plant another one. Do…do they know who did it?"

She touched my hand. "Let's not dwell on it."

I nodded, swallowing stiffly.

She smiled then. "We heard back from the scholarship people," she said. "You got in. I'm so proud of you."

*

I reach out to the package and my hands are trembling. The paper tears like soft leaves. Beneath it, is a painting. One of Sarah's best. It's the apple tree she loved. I can read the plaque at the bottom, by the roots. The detail of the bark extends right up to the gash. It's the ring-barked tree. The dying tree. But this is different: the branches of this tree are sprinkled with buds of pink and green. Death and life. This is the prize painting of her collection. It sums up her work.

And there, in the bark-stripped wood, where it never was, is my tag.

Everyone has regrets. Everyone has old wounds. Sometimes there are people who understand us even when we don't understand ourselves. This story came partly from looking back at my own pain and growth, and partly from working as a counsellor with young people struggling with difficult home lives and hoping to make something better for their lives.

BANSHEE

She felt the vision coming. It built in her throat, choking the corporeal form she'd taken, then vibrated on her tongue and burst from her lips, uncontained and raw. It would be heard for miles – by the owls in the forest to her right, by the field mice in the moors on her left, the worms in the earth and the humans in the village behind her. They would all hear it, but only she could see. In the midst of her wail, she saw what was to come: a falling ladder, a skull cracked and bleeding, ichor and glassy eyes.

When it was over, she let herself sit, digging her fingers absently into the mud and dead leaves beside the path. She would have to choose from the village. There wasn't another settlement near enough to reach before the pressure became unbearable. And they'd know it had been her.

She shouldn't have stopped there. They'd seen immediately what she was, or at least they'd suspected. She'd endured their looks as she walked into town; a mysterious woman, traveling alone with no fear. "Fey," they'd whispered, telling their children to keep close. The more cautious spread salt on their doorsteps and hung themselves with iron. It wouldn't be enough to protect them against a foretelling. She would have to choose one of them to take the death she'd seen.

She thought of the innkeeper, who had been pleasant to her gold, his greed the only thing strong enough to disguise his distrust. Humans considered it discourteous to visit death upon a host, but she'd long since given up such notions. Or she could choose one of the women who had cursed her in the street. Perhaps she should go back and try to discover which of the men in the village beat their wives and children. She could delay fate for a day or two.

She abandoned the corporeal form and shifted into a faint ball of light, glimpsed only from the corner of the eye or at a distance. Now they'd heard her wail, the villagers would not be pleased to see her face again. The wisp was a far safer form.

Night had fallen and the village was quiet when she floated into the lane. For a moment, she considered her own home. There were fewer of her kind in the world now. The great arches of the forests sang less often. There were those, such as the Banshee, who were bound to walk the world with the new race, but others slipped away and did not return.

The town square was just as empty. She sighed and her wisp-light flickered. The humans had taken to their beds. There would be nothing to learn from observing them now and there was too much iron in the village to remain until morning. The innkeeper then. It would be him.

She let the wail build in her again, intentional this time, and channeled. She saw the vision again in her breath, the face clearly that of the innkeeper. His eyes bulged with surprise as the rickety ladder swayed beneath him. The rung cracked and splintered. His foot slipped. His hand dropped the bow he'd been holding, reached for the guttering, and missed.

She turned, realising he fell from the other side of the square and saw with two visions as he toppled. His head hit the cobbles and split open, the quiver on his back spilled arrows across the square. A woman ran from the inn, adding her own wail to the noise.

She fell silent, the choice made, and watched a moment longer. She felt sad for the woman. Felt ill, in fact. A foretelling and choosing could tire her, but this was more. When the humans emerged from buildings and alleyways to surround the square, she understood. Iron.

The women raised pots and pans in their hands and the men held pitchforks and bars. All were draped with chains. They had gathered as much of the hated metal as they could get their hands on, and they'd waited. This was a trap.

The iron bit into her power and forced her back to corporeal form, the protection of the wisp banished.

"Murdering fairy," a voice hissed.

"I am only a servant of Fate," she began. An iron arrowhead thudded into her shoulder. She cursed and ripped it from her flesh before it could poison her blood. "I can give you gold."

"Gold that turns to leaves in the morning?" sneered a tall man, a pitchfork in one hand and several garden implements hanging from his belt. "I think not."

She held her hand out toward him, willing just a glimmer of power to give her light to frighten him. "Beware!"

The blow to the back of her head knocked her to her knees. The next burned the flesh of her arm and slammed her to the pavement. After that, all was pain.

When she woke, it was to old pain, not new. A soft ache. She was still burned, cut and bruised, but her wounds were bound with cloth. Her eyes flickered, but did not open. Beneath her was the spun cloth of a human home but she could feel forest around them for miles. This was not the village.

A deep, masculine voice spoke. "They gave you quite a beating, I'm afraid. Dragged you behind a horse and left you on the roadside. But your fever's broken now and that's a good sign. Don't try to talk, though; I think your jaw's cracked."

She concentrated harder, and opened her eyes. A man of maybe twenty-five stood over her. His face was blunt and tanned, his hair and eyes both dark as forest earth. Above him, was the thatched ceiling of a small cottage.

She watched his face as she said, "I heal fast."

He raised an eyebrow. "Even from iron?"

She turned her gaze away. She hadn't thought to disguise her elongated pupils. She wasn't sure she could have if she tried.

A woman came into view with a bowl of soup. She had the same blunt face and dark hair as the man but a little more youth. She placed the soup beside the bed and stepped back.

The man spoke again. "My name is Callum and this is my sister, Brigid. You'll meet our little brother Niall when he gets back from gathering firewood. Do you have a name we may call you?"

Interesting. He hadn't asked for her true-name but he had given theirs. Perhaps he believed he did not need her name to bind her, injured as she was. Her lips twisted. "Three wishes or a pot of gold?"

Callum shook his head. "Decent folk don't ask payment for common kindness."

She laughed, despite the pain. "Decent folk indeed. You're an odd human, friend Callum. And your sister, too. Perhaps I can find a way to express my thanks when I'm well."

He shook his head. "Just rest."

She closed her eyes and let her senses sink into the land. Nearest the cottage was a small farm plot, just enough for this family. Then forest. A little further to the East, the land dropped sharply, its dominion taken by the sea.

The bang of the door and a boy's voice brought her awareness back to the cottage.

"Callum! I buried all the iron like you told me and brought some wood in. Can I see the lady fairy?"

It was Brigid that answered. "No, Niall. Let her sleep."

She could feel the boy's eyes boring into her skin. She opened hers and met his gaze. He was a younger version of Callum, about nine years old, all energy and excitement – but also pain. She looked deeper and saw why. Both parents lost to sickness in less than a year, their memories treasured, but blurred. They'd left the cottage to die in the woods rather than risk their children. She closed her eyes.

A week later, she was able to conjure gold and sent Callum to the village to purchase paints. When he returned, she painted the couple she'd seen in Niall's memory: a beautiful woman with Callum's dark eyes and Brigid's burnished hair, and a strong-jawed man with rough hands. When she was done, it was lifelike in a way no mortal painter could match.

"I cannot return your parents to you," she told Niall, "but I can make sure you never forget them."

Later, Brigid came to give her soup and to say she'd seen the painting. "That was a very kind thing you did. Thank you."

"Consider it my payment," she said, but she had meant it as a gift.

Brigid sat on the edge of the bed and smiled. "I'll tell you about our parents, if you like. Then, if you should ever see them…you know…in another place…you can tell them we love them."

She smiled at the strange ideas mortals had and listened to the memories she'd helped preserve.

Over the next few days she began to make herself useful around the cottage by doing small things. She helped Brigid gather eggs, stacked the wood Callum chopped and sang lullabies to Niall. She was well enough to leave, but she enjoyed the simple pleasure of company and acceptance and was not yet ready to give it up. After all, she told herself, she was still weak.

Niall had just offered to find her some flowers when she felt her throat spasm. The wail of foretelling spewed from her mouth, uncontrolled and untempered by affections. In her breath she saw bare feet lifting from the earth, a figure tumbling from a cliff, and blood mingling with salty spray on ocean rocks.

When her sight returned to the current surroundings, Niall was staring at her, his eyes wide.

"Niall, I believe you offered to pick the lady some flowers." Callum's eyes were darker than usual as he patted his brother's shoulder. "Go and see to it."

The boy disappeared into the forest, quick as a rabbit.

She stared at the ground, her mind tumbling the options. The village was too far to have heard it. She hadn't felt any other homes nearby. Perhaps she hadn't sent her senses far enough? Perhaps there was a vagrant passing through?

There was a movement in the doorway. "Save us all," Brigid breathed. "She's a banshee."

"My lady," Callum knelt quietly beside her, "I heard that sound before the death of my parents. Can you tell me what it means?"

She shook her head but spoke the words anyway. "Someone will fall. There'll be an accident and one of you will die."

"A fall?" Callum stood suddenly and yelled into the forest. "Niall! Come back! Now!" She touched his sleeve and he turned back to her. "Is he safe? Is it him?"

"I-I don't know yet. I have to…I have to…" She bit back the last word, "choose." If she told him, he would want the choice himself. Like his parents, he would sacrifice himself to keep the family safe. She shook her head. How could she choose between them?

How did one choose?

"My lady?"

She stood, slowly and touched his face. "I was mistaken," she lied. "I thought it was a foretelling, but it wasn't. There's nothing to worry about. I just need a few minutes to walk."

The grass brushed roughly on the soles of her feet as she hurried away, then the scratch of the undergrowth, and finally the stone of the cliffs. The glamour she wove behind her made sure no one followed her.

Far below, the ocean swirled against rocks, throwing up a salty spray. She paused for a moment and thought of home. Then her feet left the earth as her wail burst forth, and she chose.

This was the first of my stories to be nominated for a Sir Julius Vogel Award after being published in JAAM issue 26. It was nominated by award winning author, Helen Lowe.

I loved the concept of the banshee giving a death warning but wondered how it would feel to be one. How would someone cope with the sense of responsibility? Then, to increase the responsibility, I changed the myth to make the banshee's part in it even stronger.

ANAESTHESIA

"Can she wake up today?" The girl's father looked up at Sally, eyes dark and untouched by the fluorescent light that glinted on the chrome bedrails.

His daughter's black hair and glitter nail-polish were a stark contrast to pallid sheets and plain taupe walls.

Sally checked the girl's vitals although she knew the nurses had already done it. The tube kept her breathing, the drip kept her asleep. The scent of lavender imperfectly masked the harsh disinfectant smell. Sally decided not to notice.

"I'm sorry." Sally shook her head and straightened her white coat over a fuchsia blouse and beige skirt. "It's best we keep her in the coma while she heals. It's her body's best chance for dealing with what's happened."

A tear slid from the mother's eye. "She's missed so much school. Her friends…She's only fourteen!"

Fourteen was an awkward age, Sally recalled, full of conflict and confusion. She left her memories with the sleeping girl and pulled the door closed behind her. A

98

nurse waited expectantly in the hall.

"Same dosage as before," Sally said. "Let's keep her under. She shouldn't feel a thing."

Her day blurred quickly after that. A general for a woman getting her appendix out. A semi-sedation for a man having a colonoscopy.

"So I'll be awake but not remember it?" he asked.

"That's right." Sally's passion-berry lips formed a smile. "Some things are best forgotten, hmm?"

*

She went home between shifts and James wanted to talk.

"Let's not," Sally told him. "Let's just get back to normal."

"Normal?" He shook his head. "You mean sleepwalking through life as if nothing touches you? That's not normal."

"Well, what would you have us do?"

"You walked in on it, for Christ's sake!" James was red in the face. His hands shook and grasped at the air. "You walked in on us and – *nothing*! Don't you feel anything?"

Sally scowled. "Of course I do. But I don't see the sense in dwelling on it. What's past is past."

His hands shook even more. "Oh my God, you're so fucking cold!" He turned, then turned back. "What if it's not past? What if it keeps going? What if every time you work late, I fuck the nanny? Would you feel anything then? Would you even give a shit?"

Sally's chest was tight. "I don't need to hear this. I'm going back to work. I'll pick up Matthew from soccer practice on my way home. Please be calm when we get in."

She was at the door with her car keys when James spoke again. "It's called football now. You don't even know what sport your son plays."

She took a deep breath. "I'll see you when we get back."

That afternoon she had coffee with Rebecca, one of the few nurses she felt comfortable with. A little of the foam and sprinkled cinnamon had drizzled down the side of Rebecca's latte cup.

"So how are things with you and James?" Rebecca asked.

Sally's cup was perfect. "We're fine," she said. "Really great. Of course, we're both so busy with work, there's no time for troubles really." She smiled widely. "And Matthew's doing well at school. He's in the soccer team now – football, I think they're calling it these days." She took a sip from her cappuccino.

Rebecca rolled her eyes. "Sports! It starts now and then it's all they think about for the rest of their lives!"

"Too true." Sally chuckled, lips stretched into a smile.

Rebecca ran a finger around the rim of her cup, wiping away some of the spilled foam. "Hey, you know there've been some questions about the girl in the medically induced coma?"

Sally nodded. "Her parents have been asking for a second opinion. They don't understand why we're keeping her under so long."

Rebecca nodded. "The thing is, some of the doctors are wondering as well."

"Is that so?"

Rebecca spread her hands innocently. "I just thought you should know."

Sally stood up. "Thanks. I'd better get back."

*

The needle penetrated the patient. She pressed too hard and he winced. She pushed the plunger and his pain was gone.

Get rid of pain or mask it. That was her job. She helped people to be unconscious to the inner workings of themselves, to not feel their pain as infection or cancer was cut out, to not scream in the face of what needed to be done. She protected that poor girl from having to face what had happened to her. She kept her safe. How could anyone question that?

The patient mumbled, his arm twitching as the drugs took over. His hand brushed her thigh and she jumped back. "He's ready."

"Sally." Rebecca's voice was harsh, somehow thicker than usual. Her eyebrows were taut as sutures. "Sally, there's been an accident at Matt's school. He's downstairs in the ER."

"But…" She frowned at the vial in her hand. Her heart thumped painfully. "But…"

Rebecca took the vial from her hand and placed it on the tray. "You need to deal with Matt. I'll take over from here." Rebecca gave her a little shove toward the door. "Go!"

She heard James's voice again her mind, "so fucking cold," and she ran.

*

She strode across the concrete, the sound of her shoes like castanets: clack-clack clack-clack clack-clack.

Too fast. She gripped the car remote in stiff fingers. Bloody ER doctors! It was a broken arm! A broken arm and they'd had her thinking the worst. She saw broken bones every day and coped sensibly. But today...today her body trembled and she couldn't slow her steps. She punched the button on the remote with her thumb and heard the comforting bleep-bleep in the distance.

Matthew trailed her, his neon-blue cast peeping from within the gauze sling. His knees were scuffed and muddy and his socks were grass-stained. He carried his sports bag over his good shoulder.

She reached the car before he did and stared at her reflection in the window. A strand of her hair had come loose. She raised her hand to tuck it back in place, but then let it drop. The eyes that stared back at her were dark and deep and tired. The carefully applied makeup hid any sign of bags, but she couldn't hide the rest any more.

Matthew came up beside her. Quietly, he said, "Coach says it's okay to cry, you know."

"Really?" She looked at him and forced her lips into a smile. "Does he say that?"

Matt nodded enthusiastically, then winced as the movement jostled his sling.

Sally frowned. "Does your arm hurt?"

"Yeah, but not as much as before."

"Didn't they give you anything for the pain? Bloody ER doctors!"

Matt rolled his eyes. "Mum! I said I didn't want anything."

"What? Why?"

He shrugged his one good shoulder. "It's not so bad

now. And if I can't feel the pain, how will I know when it's getting better?"

"Oh." Sally's skin tingled in a wave of pins and needles. Suddenly the sun felt very warm. She thought of James. "Oh." Her tired eyes felt wet.

"Mum? You okay?"

She took a deep breath and patted him awkwardly on the back. "Yeah. Get in the car and let's go home to Dad."

When he'd closed the door behind him, Sally took out her cell-phone and made a call. "Tell the family to be ready in the morning. It's time for her to wake up."

Like the character in this story, one of my coping strategies when I'm hurt is to shut down. I liken it to having a big red button that slams up the shields. It's a strategy that works sometimes but the danger is being trapped behind those shields and not letting anyone else in. Staying numb. Staying anaesthetised. That's a good way to miss out on life.

DRAG MARKS

When the zombie apocalypse hit, I was in a gay bar. In drag.

The world changed that night. And I wasn't ready.

An outfit including glittering, eight inch heels is not designed for running from the undead. That's a real eight inches too, not the ever-hopeful, cyberspace measurement you see in internet hook-up profiles. I could barely walk in them, let alone run.

The club was packed with guys, queens and even the occasional biological woman. Shirtless shot-boys carried trays of tiny glasses between handsy bears and dancing twinks, but the real attraction was on the stage. Drag night was always a hit. The queens here were among the best in town. They always loosened up the crowd and made people laugh. And who doesn't want to let their stress and inhibitions go at the end of the week?

Especially a week where the news was full of some new virus straining hospital resources.

The guy beside me whistled as the next queen sashayed on stage. It practically pierced my eardrum.

"Wow, dude, use your inside voice."

He looked me over and gave a little shrug.

I resisted the urge to straighten my wig. I was pretty sure some of it was tangled in my earrings again, but Karl always said you should maintain the illusion when in public. "Don't piece it together in front of everyone. If your look is busted, then take it out back or own it."

I didn't want to miss the show so I figured I'd have to own it.

The whistler took a swig of his beer. "That girl is serving fish on a platter tonight."

I snorted. Ultra-feminine in drag? That's my Karl. "He always does. He'd take out the trash in heels if I let him."

Whistler's eyes widened. "Carmen Ovami is your boyfriend?" He looked me over again.

Why did I let Karl convince me to do drag? He always does it so much better than I do.

I opened my mouth to make a smart remark, but that's when the woman stumbled up. Her skin was ashen and her eyes were already bloodshot. Her hand clamped to the side of her neck, her mouth worked as though she were chewing the words on their way out. "Someone...bit me."

Her jaw fell slack and her head lolled to one side. The arm at her neck dropped away and blood dripped from a hole the size of a human mouth. Dripping, not flowing or spurting like it should be if a chunk of flesh were bitten away. A convulsion ran through her body like an electric pulse and then she was still.

The guy beside me swore. "What the fuck?"

Then the screams started.

106

My eyes scanned the crowd now surging like spooked cattle. A group of grey-skinned people were advancing from the door. The bouncer was on his knees, clutching his shoulder. Two or three other people had fallen, the grey-skinned newcomers bending over them on the floor. No, not bending over them – feeding on them! They took bites of their flesh while their victims screamed.

I turned back to the woman who'd been attacked. Her eyes were almost completely glazed red now, and she lunged forward, latching her mouth onto Whistler's forearm. He yelped and tried to shake her off, but she clung tight. Blood ran from the corners of her mouth as she bit deep.

"Shit!" My mind ran back to the media coverage of the viral outbreak. Pale and clammy, bloodshot eyes, confused with dementia-like symptoms. No fucking kidding. "It's a plague."

"Jason. Jason!" Karl's voice boomed across the screams, deep and crisp. He must be scared, I thought, to use his boy voice while in drag.

Whistler's face had drained pale. He fell to the floor. More of the grey faces piled on top of him.

I ran to the stage, toward Karl's voice. My breath fluttered in my chest and my stomach lurched. They were trying to *eat people*.

My feet wobbled in the stupid heels and the panicked patrons jostled me. I swore as my ankle twisted and I nearly fell. My wig was definitely crooked now. Karl yelled again. I almost didn't hear him, people screaming all around me. "Shit." I paused to pull off the shoes and continued in stockinged feet.

Almost immediately, some idiot stood on my toes. "Fuck!"

I'd almost reached the stage when something grabbed my leg. I looked down. It was one of them. He lay on the floor, his body bloody and trampled, the lower half mostly gone, torn away. But he kept moving. His fingers were locked around my leg. He dragged himself forward, red eyes wide, head tilted to the side, and opened his mouth to take a bite of my calf.

I swung the shoes. The heels sank into his skull like the soft shell of an Easter egg. He let go and I jerked back. Gore pulled out with the shoes.

I stumbled away, horrified.

Then Karl was there. In drag he was always glamorous. Beautiful hair, sequined dress, shining lips. But when he pulled me into a hug, the femininity of Carmen was gone. He held on tight and hard.

"Thank God, you're okay." He pulled back and looked me over. "Jesus, what did you do to those shoes? You know how much they cost?"

I gestured around us at the chaos. "Seriously? Not the time."

He nodded, those glittering red lips pressed tight. He'd used the coloured lashes tonight and it really made his blue eyes pop. "You're right. There's an exit back stage."

He grabbed my hand and we ran. Past bodies being torn apart, through the dressing room, where a yellow-haired drag queen, Sam, was fending off zombies with a blowtorch improvised from can of hairspray. Under layers of concealer, Sam still had a military tattoo. He and his boyfriend had met in the army, he'd once told me. He gestured towards us with sharp, marine-like jabs, a silver bracelet of musical theatre charms jingling like fairy alarm bells on his wrist. "The back door! Go for the car park."

"Thanks." We ran out into Hell, all the way home.

The last TV broadcast we ever saw tried to explain it. The new virus had mutated further, infecting the living and animating the dead. If you were bitten, you were one of them. If you were lucky. Otherwise, they tore you apart and ate your flesh.

"It's an honest to god zombie apocalypse."

Karl and I watched the city burn from our balcony. Apartment living had its advantages. Security swipe cards to get into the lobby. Elevators to get to the upper floors. No one in the suburbs had a chance. One-level comfy family homes with a yard – easy pickings.

In the first few days, the emergency services tried to respond. Then the army. The numbers were too great. There were too few of us left.

"I wish we had a gun." Karl squeezed my hand. The wigs and makeup were gone now. He wore a singlet and the ring I'd given him around his neck on a chain - it was too masculine for Carmen but he never liked to be without it.

I stared at the streets below. Even at a distance I could tell who was still human and who was not. The slow, dragging pace of the infected gave them away less than the terrified running of those still fighting for their lives. They were mostly on foot now. The roads were too clogged with abandoned cars for anything else. Windscreens did nothing to keep out a zombie.

"You seriously think you could shoot somebody in

the head?"

I felt his shrug more than saw it. "If I had to. Maybe."

I bit my lip and turned to stare at him. "They're sick, Karl. They have a virus. A *virus* makes them like this. You wanna shoot me next?"

Realisation sparked in his eyes. "That's different, babe. I get that you want them cured but look at what they're doing. They're eating people. They don't have any mind left. They're not human any more."

I turned and walked back inside. "Some people felt that way about me."

He called after me. "I didn't."

The apartment was a mess. Karl's makeup and wig collection were scattered throughout the bathroom, bedroom and living area – but that was nothing new. We'd not tidied in days. Three bags of rubbish waited by the door. Neither of us was brave enough to leave the apartment to remove them, and I refused to simply throw them over the balcony. Some small part of me clung to civilised ideas like recycling and not being a litterbug.

Empty cans of food and candy wrappers were everywhere. Early on we'd raided the dairy on the ground floor of our building and taken everything we could find to eat. There was no hope of fresh produce now, but the canned vegetables, frozen curries, and chocolate had kept us going. I'd intended to pay for it all when things returned to normal. I'd even made a list of what we'd taken. But things like that weren't important anymore.

The TV was nothing but static now. It had been for days. I flicked it off. There was no point waiting for messages that would never come. TV and radio stations weren't broadcasting anymore. We were lucky we still had electricity.

As the white-noise faded and the screen turned to black, something else reached my ears. A voice inside the building.

"Help! Somebody help! Fire!"

A jolt ran through me. Screams were commonplace now, but this was close. Very close. I pressed my ear to the door.

"Please! Somebody!" There was a catch in the voice I couldn't ignore.

I undid the lock and ran into the corridor. Swearing, Karl followed me out and grabbed my elbow.

"What are you doing?"

I pulled away. "Listen."

"It'll be one of them," he said. "A zombie."

"They can't talk. You know that."

The voice called again. This time it was clearly a woman's voice, coming from an apartment across the hall. "Is anyone there? I need help!" The door was ajar.

"Shit."

I pushed the door open, with Karl crowding in behind me. The apartment was the same layout as ours, but this room was tidy and precise. A single armchair sat in the corner and there was no sofa to be seen. Beside the armchair, facing the television was a large metal frame surrounding what looked like a flattened out chair with seatbelts.

A woman in a power wheelchair struggled against the door to the bedroom, which shuddered and banged against her chair. She squealed and revved the engine, driving the chair harder into the door as something tried to open it from the other side. "I can't hold it. Help!"

Karl called, "Jason, don't."

I ran forward, slamming into the door as it moved again. A low, guttural moan came from within. I pushed with all my force but could barely budge it. The woman flicked the joystick on her chair again and edged forward. The latch caught but the door shook again as the zombie inside pushed against it.

Karl dragged the armchair from the corner of the room. "Get out of the way." As he came closer, I helped him position it, holding the door closed.

Finally, we fell back, exhausted.

Karl turned on the woman. She wore stretchy dark pants and a knitted jumper. Her dark hair was dishevelled and she was out of breath. "Why is there a zombie in your bedroom?"

She twitched the joystick and her chair rotated to face him. "Why do you think? I wanted a pet and the store was out of kittens." She looked us over. "You're the gays from across the hall."

Karl scowled. "And you're the cripple."

I caught my breath but the woman chuckled. "Touché. I'm Alison." She tilted her head toward the blocked door. "That was Danielle, my carer. She must have been bitten on our food run, poor girl."

I stared. "You go outside?"

She nodded, patting the chair controls. "I can outrun any zombie in this thing. I get their attention and Danielle grabs the stuff." She paused and stared at the floor. "I guess she got caught on the way back. She started turning before we even got inside."

A part of me knew I should be more upset by that. Another innocent person infected and destroyed. A kind, caring person who looked after someone in a wheelchair. But somehow I couldn't let it touch me. All my friends were gone now. What was one more woman lost in the crowd?

"You probably shouldn't stay here now. Take one of the other apartments. There's hardly anyone left any more. We can help you move your..." I waved at the metal and chair contraption.

"It's a standing frame. Leave it. I can't get in and out of it alone anyway."

I didn't know what to say to that.

Alison took a deep breath. "Look, I don't want to ask this but you're the only people I know left...without Danielle, I'll need someone to help me. I have muscular dystrophy. I can't get out of this chair by myself or lift my arms more than this." She raised them just a few inches above the chair's armrests.

"What kind of help?" I moved across to the kitchen area and leaned against the bench.

"Getting in and out of the chair," Alison said. "Food preparation. Getting into bed, or going to the bathroom..."

Karl threw up his hands. "Oh, hell no."

"I can't do it alone," Alison said. There was a note of desperation in her voice.

I shook my head. "Karl, we can't leave her."

He looked as if he would argue, but then he frowned. "Babe, you're bleeding."

I looked at my arm. A long graze on my forearm ran red. "It's not a bite. I scraped it on the door."

Karl came towards me but I jerked back.

"Don't touch it."

He went still. "Why not?"

I turned away. "You know why."

Behind me, he sighed. I ignored it, picking up a tea towel and pressing it against the cut. When I turned back around, Alison was watching us with narrowed eyes.

"Ah, crap," she said. "That's all I need. You boys have HIV?"

I stared at the tea towel. Spots of red appeared in the beige pattern. "I do. Karl's clean."

Alison said, "Ah, well. Beggars can't be choosers. Throw that towel out when you're done with it."

Karl jumped to my defence. "He's on medication and has an undetectable viral load. He's perfectly healthy and safe to be around so you can take your judgement and stick it up your arse."

I shut my eyes and took a deep breath. "Karl," I said.

He kept talking. "I'm so sick of uneducated people."

"Karl!" I raised my head, trying to put what I was feeling into my face.

"What?" He softened when he saw my expression. "What is it?"

"I'm out of meds."

His mouth worked soundlessly before he found the words. "As of when?"

"I took the last one yesterday."

He was quiet for a long moment. "That's okay. It's still in your system. You haven't even missed any yet.

We just need to get more. We'll go to the pharmacy."

I shook my head. "We can't. You've seen what the streets are like out there. How do we get that far and back safely?"

Alison wheeled forward in her chair. "I've been out there," she said. "Lots of times. If you help me with the things I need, I'll help you get your meds."

Karl and I looked at each other. There was no need to say it out loud. Without those meds, my viral load would rise out of control. Eventually, not right away, but eventually, I would die. Horribly.

I swallowed and dropped the tea towel on the bench. "Deal."

We spent the next three hours discussing how best to get across six city blocks and a bridge to the pharmacy without being killed or infected by the zombies.

"We need a disguise," Karl said. "What if I do us up as zombies? I have the makeup. We can make our faces grey, put on some fake wounds and rotting skin. They never try to eat each other – if they think we're one of them maybe they'll leave us alone."

It was the best we could come up with.

I put on a dirty, torn-up long-sleeved top and jeans, and Karl painted every exposed part of my skin to look grey and bloody. Then he went to work on himself. Not satisfied with coming along as Karl, he put fake blood on one of his wigs and transformed himself into a zombie version of his drag-self, Carmen. He wore a torn sundress and smudged lipstick that clashed with the fake blood of the painted on wounds.

"You don't have to come with us," I said, watching him.

Karl smiled and patted my cheek. "Of course I do. I'm not letting you get eaten without me."

I bit my lip. There was no stopping him when he was like this. "Well, you're not doing it in heels."

His eyes twinkled. "Not even the gold glitter pumps?"

"Definitely not."

He leaned in and kissed me on the cheek. "Okay, babe. Running shoes it is."

The streets were quieter around mid-afternoon. Something about the heat of the day slowed the zombies down. Perhaps the warmth accelerated the decomposition of their wounds. Perhaps there was still just enough human left in them to feel lethargic and in need of a nap. Whatever it was, Alison assured us this was a good time to move.

"I'll go ahead," she said. "I move faster than you anyway. I'll draw them away, then circle back to you. While I'm gone, just try to stay out of sight and move like they do."

My breath felt hot and tight, as though it was being squeezed out of me. Getting enough air seemed impossible. I watched as Alison's power wheelchair whizzed ahead of us, winding between stationary cars as she left the footpath and took to the road. Several zombies appeared from the surrounding buildings and lurched after her, moaning like undead cows.

"Come on, motherfuckers," Alison yelled. "Come and get me."

My legs felt heavy and weak. I moved forward, the shuffling stagger of the zombies coming more from fear than design. "Shit, shit, shit." I kept a steady stream of profanity under my breath.

Carmen brushed my shoulder as he passed. His dress fluttered in the breeze, yellow and orange sunflowers. He carried a white lace parasol, closed, in one hand. "It's okay," he said quietly. "Move a little faster. We can do this."

His touch lit up something inside me. The tightness in my chest relax and my feet were mine once more. I gave a slight nod, and followed as Carmen led the way, dragging one foot a little, as though infected. Something sparkled on the pavement and I fought a chuckle. He'd worn his running shoes but glued glitter to the soles – they left scuff marks of shiny Karl-ness whenever he dragged his foot.

"Idiot," I whispered. I let my head loll to the side and tried to mimic his way of walking.

Two blocks felt like a marathon. Alison and her comet-tail of zombies had vanished and we were reaching the edge of the cleared area she'd left behind. A grey-skinned man with half his face sliced away stepped out from a shadowed doorway. I fought the urge to grab Karl's hand.

The half-face stared blankly as we passed, making no move to follow.

A block later, three more zombies crossed the road in front of us. Then another stopped and watched us coming closer. His left arm hung twisted at the elbow. His forehead was a mass of sores but his red eyes stared right at us.

"It knows," I whispered. "Shit. We need to run."

Carmen slowed her pace. "Not yet. Just wait. Keep going."

I struggled to keep my face neutral as we came closer. My gaze flicked to the sides of the street. There were more zombies. More decayed faces and red eyes. Watching us.

The one with the messy forehead moaned. I breathed in. Deep. The stench of him almost overpowered the garbage in the street. Rot and blood and filth.

The high whine of a motor came from behind us. "Wait up, boys. I haven't cleared the way yet." It was Alison.

There was a thud and the motor stopped.

"Shit! I'm gonna need help."

The zombies swayed and their heads turned slowly, undead hunters scenting prey. Karl and I did the same. My breath caught in my chest.

Alison's chair was caught in a pothole. She revved it and wriggled the joystick but the chair was stuck.

The zombies advanced towards her, their moans louder, excited, hungry.

Karl and I were closer, but we didn't dare move too quickly – be too human in the sight of the other zombies. It felt like forever before we reached her, the zombies just a few steps behind.

We leaned in as if to bite her but instead pushed on the chair. "I thought you said you could outrun these zombies."

"I can if the road is wheelchair friendly! Complain to your city council." Alison threw the joystick forward, the motor screamed and the wheels skidded. "Lean on the back. Tip it so the front wheels raise."

We heaved. Messy forehead was only a few steps

away. His stench hit me again, the rot filling my lungs.

The wheelchair tipped back, just a fraction, and the front wheels caught on the lip of the pothole. Alison jerked the controls and suddenly the whole thing lurched forward.

Karl and I lost our grip and stumbled, catching ourselves just in time to see Alison zoom past the first few zombies, bumping them out of the way. She screamed obscenities, circled to make sure she had all their attention, then shot up a side road, the zombies in tow.

"That woman's crazy," I said.

The last couple of blocks before the bridge felt like miles. My ears were straining for any hint of Alison's wheelchair. It had been almost twice as long since she'd been gone the last time and still there was nothing.

The bridge was littered with zombies. They wandered aimlessly back and forth, as though confused by the walled off edges of the road. In the distance, more of them were milling in front of the pharmacy.

"What do we do?"

"She'll be back soon," Karl murmured. "Let's wait."

We loitered at the entrance to the bridge, swaying like the stationary zombies we'd seen. Then we shuffled back and forth. The glitter had worn off Karl's shoes. There was nothing between us and being killed but a thin veneer of makeup and acting. The zombies on the bridge drifted, as though somehow aware of the empty expanse behind us and wanting to spread out and fill the void.

Finally, I said what we both feared. "I don't think

she's coming back. What if she got stuck?" The incident with the pothole had shaken me up. Alison, for all her bravado, would be helpless if her chair got stuck again. She could do nothing to free herself and was incapable of fighting the zombies who would come to eat her flesh.

Karl glanced at me, fear in his eyes beneath the false lashes. He took a deep breath. "We can make it. They think we're one of them."

I swallowed. "Yeah. We can make it."

We started forward, slowly, as if it were by chance, without purpose. The first few zombies ignored us. But then we got closer. Red eyes turned to watch. A horrible thought struck me – what if Alison had deliberately left us? What if she'd never intended to keep us safe but had lured us to our doom? She knew more about their behaviour than we did, having been outside more. Maybe this was a trap?

My breathing quickened. "We should go back."

"Ssssh." Carmen said.

I turned, but the zombies had closed in behind us. We were trapped on the bridge and there were as many in front of us as there were behind. Nowhere was safe.

Carmen moved on. I was being left behind. "Karl!" I hissed. "Wait!"

A zombie stepped between us. He was shirtless. His arm had a military tattoo and a charm bracelet.

My eyes widened and I stumbled. "Sam! Fuck, it's Sam!"

The Sam zombie turned toward me. It groaned and reached out, bracelet jingling like bells. I jerked back but not quickly enough. It seized my wrist and held on.

I leaned back, pulling away from the zombie with all my strength as it leaned in. Its horrible blackened mouth opened, teeth exposed. "No! Sam, let me go!"

The handle of Carmen's lace parasol struck him in the face with an almighty crack. The zombie fell back, teeth scattering on the pavement.

Carmen struck it again and it went down, releasing my wrist as it fell. "Run!"

The other zombies had seen us fight and recognised the behaviour of prey. They moved in.

They were everywhere, lurching at us from all directions. Carmen laid about with the parasol, but all I could think of was to move forward. To run. We had to get across the bridge to the pharmacy. Maybe we could lock ourselves inside.

Up ahead, more zombies were pouring onto the bridge, drawn by our shouts. We ran. We dodged. We fought. We were failing. They crowded around us, in front and behind. There was nowhere left to run.

I waited for the sharp bite of zombie teeth on my flesh, the final signal that life was over – that this new world had beaten me. It didn't come.

"Hey, you undead dickheads! Over here!" Alison's voice boomed behind us and the zombies faltered, confused. "Come to mama!"

I dared a glance and saw zombies fall like skittles as she barrelled into them from behind. They tipped, taking others with them. The wheels of her chair crunched over a skull and a gluey mess squelched out onto the road.

She circled us, whooping as she went. "Meals on wheels, bitches. Come and get it!"

"Stay still," Carmen muttered, touching my arm.

I didn't need telling. The movement and sound of the chair had taken our attackers' attention away from us. Alison was the prey now. We were back to being one of the crowd.

"See ya!" Alison yelled, and her chair kicked into overdrive, zooming ahead of us, over the bridge. The zombies followed.

We shuffled, as slowly as we dared, bumped and jostled by the zombies as they passed us in pursuit of Alison. Finally, they'd all overtaken us and we trailed behind, unseen. She led them down another two blocks, then turned up a side road, out of sight.

I swallowed. "Like I said, she's crazy."

The door of the pharmacy was broken, a shattered hole in a frame of glass. Inside, shelves were tipped over and cold medicine, vitamins, hair clips and skin lotions warred with each other for space on the floor. Several broken bottles of bubble-bath gave the place a pungent citrus odour. We stepped gingerly over the mess and made our way deeper inside.

"Do you know where to look for it?"

I shrugged. "He always goes out the back and to the left. Let's just hope there still is some."

Carmen stayed in the shop, parasol at the ready, while I went out back. Walking into the staff-only section felt strange. The shelves were lined with bottles and boxes, each with careful labels and shiny drug company logos.

I searched for the familiar red and white box. "I think they're alphabetical," I called out. "But…maybe by drug type as well."

My limited drug knowledge recognised Augmentin and a few other antibiotics from the first couple of shelves and I moved on, muttering to myself as I went. "Avigra, Cialis, Viagra. Come on. If I were an anti-viral medication, where would I be?"

In the main part of the shop, Karl was shifting things around. Probably filling a bag with makeup, if I knew him.

Then, "Aha! Atripla." I pounced on a box and held it up in triumph. There were rows of them. "Found it."

I turned, just in time to catch a glimpse of a white coat before a sharp pain bit into the back of my neck.

I screamed and lashed out with my elbows. The zombie groaned and let go. I stumbled away, crashing into the shelves. Medicines fell in an avalanche all around me, clacking and rattling like tiny bottle castanets.

I pushed past, stumbling into the shop. I clutched my hand to my neck. It was wet. I turned back to look at the zombie who had bitten me - the pharmacist. His mouth was red with my blood, but his face was pale. He licked his lips, his eyes widened, and the red drained from them as I watched. They were blue – *human* blue.

His mouth chewed air before finally forming words. "Help me." He clutched at a rotting stomach wound and slowly slid to the floor.

I stared, shaking. It wasn't possible. Nothing stopped them once they got a taste of flesh.

Wary of being tricked, I leaned forward for a closer look. Nothing.

I kicked him. No response. The zombie was dead - properly dead - without a head-shot. If I didn't know

123

better, I'd say the wound in his stomach had killed him, but the virus animated corpses with no regard for bodily damage.

"Jason," Karl's voice was weak and thin. "Jason, I'm sorry. He got me."

I ran around the counter and saw him, sprawled against one of the toppled display shelving units. His sundress was bloody with real blood now. A chunk of flesh was missing from his arm. His wig was askew and he used some of the hair to wipe the makeup off his face. Beneath the paint, his skin was grey.

"No!" Something thudded inside my chest with the weight of Alison's wheelchair. I fell to my knees at his side.

Karl pulled away. "Leave me. Run!" His eyes were already turning bloodshot.

I shook my head. "Never."

His lip was trembling and tiny spasms rippled through his body. Tears traced mascara lines on his cheeks. "Please, babe. I'm turning into one of them. Don't let me infect you. Please!"

I stroked his face. Beneath the wig and the makeup was my Karl. My man. My queen. "He bit me too. We'll turn together."

He swallowed and I could see the strain in the muscles all the way down his neck. "Liar. Your eyes are fine. Your skin is fine. You need to run."

I frowned. I felt fine. Aside from the sting of the bite on my neck, and my terror at what was happening to Karl, physically, I felt fine.

I pulled up my sleeve – no grey skin. I should be infected by now.

I looked back at the dead zombie pharmacist. Dead for no reason. I clenched my fists and the hard edges of the Atripla box dug into my palm. Antiviral meds.

Antiviral.

"Fuck!" It hit me at last. "I have antiviral medication in my system. The zombies are made by a *virus*!" My blood had killed the virus in the pharmacist – he'd died because his body had sustained too much damage to survive without the virus animating it.

What if Karl got my blood before his body was fully changed by the zombie virus? If I could kill the virus before the virus killed him?

I lifted my arm up to his mouth. "Do it."

He tried to speak, to deny me, but words failed.

His eyes turned fully red.

His teeth sank into my flesh…

The world changed when the zombie apocalypse hit and I didn't think I was ready. It was too scary, too out of control. But as I helped Karl to his feet and we made our way home – me with my bag of meds and Karl with his makeup supplies – I realised the truth. Despite the chaos in this new world - despite the zombies and the mayhem - we were going to be okay.

We're survivors. And the world can just bite me.

Zombies have been a hot subject for a while now. Personally, I've always preferred a magic or voodoo zombie to the modern style of virus or plague zombie. The inspiration for "Drag Marks" came out of a conversation about this. Part of the issue I have is that zombies infected with a virus are technically sick and therefore it seems harsh to shoot them in the head rather than try to trap and cure them. Of course, there's always self-preservation to think of, but it's shocking how quickly the perception of humanity is stripped away. It got me thinking about what other viruses society has stigmatised and allowed to be an excuse for dehumanising people. The result is a story in which the three heroes and survivors are not what one would normally expect in a zombie apocalypse.

Double Happiness

The first stroke was smooth. The ink had just the right consistency - somewhere between Luong Tsang tea and pikelet batter. The red sable bristles bent softly but held their shape as they dragged colour across the paper.

He always thought of himself as Shi Dao when he painted. Simon was a good name – a good Kiwi name – but calligraphy required Shi Dao. Tiao still disliked that he'd taken an English name, but it made things easier here. She was happy, at least, that it was his real name that collectors looked for on his art.

The brush swooped a long, soft curve across the paper, like a long, sweeping drive, all unblemished concrete and manicured hedges. He remembered how Tiao had chirped and preened when they'd visited the Tiangs. "Did you see how that David looked at Amanda?" Her seatbelt was the only rumple in her blouse. "He's a good boy. Amanda, did you hear he's going to medical school?"

"Mmmm." Amanda's response barely reached them from the back seat. Her attention was already split between headphones and a chemistry textbook.

The ink curved and shaped the story. A family with a good home, community respect, and a son going to medical school. Good prospects. The brush flicked the final few lines in place. This was "prosperity".

He pulled the paper aside to dry, and reached for a fresh sheet. This time, the character would be "love". He knew exactly what memories would go into this painting. He wet the brush quickly, and remembered.

Si Tiao's dress had been red like rubies. She was young, then, full of life, and so was he. A painter too taken with Western styles to be a success in China, he'd had no right to claim her.

"I'm going to New Zealand, Tiao." His hand reached out of its own accord, almost touching, but not quite, the smooth beauty of her cheek. "They say I could make a better life there. My work will be exotic. They're not as structured as here."

Her face was marble. No lip quiver or tears, but he could tell her breath had stopped. Her dark mirror eyes reflected his own turmoil.

"Your father is right, Tiao. I'm not a good match for you. Not here. But in New Zealand…maybe I could be. Will you come?"

The brush flourished upward on the curl. This was happiness as well as love. He moved the paint to a new character, "double happiness", the traditional wedding symbol. Interwoven with "love", they would make each other strong.

He reached for another memory, but reality intruded.

"I'm capable of choosing my own boyfriends, mother!"

Shi Dao's hand paused mid-stroke. He finished the line quickly, but the mark of hesitation was there.

"Amanda, this is not about choosing boyfriends." Tiao's voice was almost reasonable – with just a hint of shrillness. "It's about maturity. It's about doing what's right for you and your family. You're old enough to be responsible and that boy is simply not suitable. Now, the Tiang's son-"

"David is an idiot."

"He's in medical school!"

"That's the only reason you like him, Mother! He's boring, self-absorbed-"

"A doctor can provide for you better than a guitar player who has no idea about our ways!"

Amanda's voice lowered. "He knows *my* ways. More than you. Anyway, it's about love."

Simon looked around. These two would argue a while yet unless he could find something to distract them. He sighed. Like mother like daughter. No simpering flower would have defied her father to come with him to a strange land. He picked up the half-finished painting. He would ask their opinion and redirect them both.

"You should know," Amanda insisted. "You married Dad for love instead of the rich guy your parents wanted."

"Yes! And look where that got me!"

The world shrank for a moment. Simon's hand clenched. His breath was shallow.

"I'd have been much better off if I'd done as my parents wanted! Don't be a fool, Amanda. Marry a doctor."

Simon stepped into the room. He could not see his wife's face. Amanda's was set hard, her lips thin. "If I marry, it'll be who I choose." She turned like a soldier and marched away, doors slamming like gunshots behind her.

Tiao moved to follow but Simon touched her arm. "Was it really such a bad decision, Tiao?"

She paused a long moment, brushed at her dress, then turned to face him. "I could have had better than this."

He closed his eyes against the words. "You should have told me. I'd have done differently."

Her laugh was a bark. "Admit that love was not enough? What kind of wife would I be then?"

He nodded as the world they'd shared splintered. "I see," he said at last, and turned back to the studio. The crumpled painting slipped from his fingers, unnoticed, and was lost.

"Double Happiness" was the first of my stories to win a prize, taking second place in a national competition at a book festival. I travelled four hours to read it aloud – something I was terrified to do at the time!

The inspiration came in part from having seen the breakdown of relationships with my parents and in part from frustration with how my writing had been received up until then. It was my first foray into a more literary style without fantasy elements. While I've never given up on speculative fiction as a genre, I found I enjoyed writing literary short fiction and it helped develop my skills.

LOYALTY

The captain's wife had a silver turbine gem at the nape of her neck. Gafin traced the shape with his fingers. The edge burrowed into her skin, tapping into veins so the turbine within whirled in response to her heartbeat, a tiny wheel turning beneath the resin, converting pulse to kinetic energy for her implants.

She shifted and the sheet slipped lower down her back. "That feels nice."

Gafin smiled. "Good." He ran his finger down the hard edge and onto her soft skin. The pleasure of her company had a bite of guilt. Six more months until they were anywhere near a civilised space dock. More if the captain decided there was another potential salvage out here. It was a long time to keep sneaking around. "Hennah," he began.

The ship's computer sounded an alert, the invasive chime battering at his languid mood like a boarding ram. He glanced at the screen on the wall. *Crew storage chamber unlocked. Cryogenic dehibernation sequence active: Pod 9.* Except two of the letters were blocked out by unrecognisable symbols, like a censorship sticker melted over the glass.

"Piece of crap system," he muttered. "How long has it been since we had an upgrade?"

Hennah sat up, holding the sheet across her breasts. "What's going on?"

"Your husband's on the move. We better get dressed."

She frowned. "Really? I could've sworn he'd be in the lab with those artefacts for days yet."

Gafin nodded toward the screen. "He's set Pawl defrosting. I guess he needs a hand."

"And he didn't think to ask those of us who are actually on duty." She let herself flop back onto the pillow. "Typical."

Gafin frowned. "Has your translation programme finished yet?"

"No. So it's a waste of time waking any of the others. We can't access any of the salvage logs or read his precious book until we decode the language."

He shrugged, leaning in to kiss her shoulder. "You know what he's like. He loves doing things the old-fashioned way."

That was another good reason to get dressed and check things out. The captain was likely to run the dehibernation manually. As medical officer, Gafin had a responsibility to the crew to make sure they came out of it okay.

He glanced at the computer screen again. "Oh shit!" A chill filled his stomach. One of the screen glitch blobs was sitting just before the 9. He leapt out of bed and pulled on his trousers, not even stopping for underwear. "It's not Pod 9. It's Pod19."

Hennah swore. She pulled a long shirt over her head, covering her to about mid-thigh, and ran from the room.

Gafin pressed his fingers to the communication implant at the back of his jaw. "Captain, you need to stop dehibernation on Pod 19. That's Marc. If we wake him, he'll die. Captain?"

Rough static and an indecipherable whisper answered. Another glitch in the ship's system.

Marc had been a casualty of the last salvage, an abandoned alien vessel floating in the void with enough new technology to make a very healthy pay day – if they could figure out what it was for and how to work it.

It'd taken three weeks to clear it all safely into the lab. Any time they were dealing with unknown tech there were safety protocols to be followed. Anything could be a potential danger. More often than not something that looked dangerous turned out to be the alien equivalent of a music player or a toaster but they never knew what might trigger a self-destruct sequence. A salvage where the alien crew were all dead was even more fraught.

They'd downloaded the logs and taken what books and equipment they could but Marc had been certain there was more. "These ships almost always have a secret hold," he'd said. "For smuggling valuables or whatever. It's worth a bit of extra time to find it. The crew killed each other over something. What's the bet it was for better shares of the loot?"

He'd found his secret door all right – but it was an

airlock for a personal lifepod that was absent when he popped the seal. The resulting decompression and the suction from the vacuum of space left him with a severe head injury and nothing that could be done but freeze him 'til they returned to dock. There was a limit to how much Gafin could do for injuries in space.

The door to the infirmary was open when Gafin got there. Hennah was stopped just outside. Cryopods lined the centre of the room like the median strip on a highway. Only a handful of crew were out of hibernation and on duty at any time unless there was something to actually work on so the majority of the pods were full. Two were open.

"*Picell nok draguul.*" A whispery voice came from inside. "*Picell nok draguul.*"

Gafin followed the voice inside.

Marc was already awake and standing beside an open cryopod. His pupils were huge and black. His lips moved as he spoke the alien words. He stared into the pod, at the stirring figure within.

Gafin glanced at the screen on the wall. *Cryogenic dehibernation sequence active: Pod 15.* More of the letters were obliterated by the strange symbols this time, but he could read enough to know who was in the pod. Marc's wife, Serra.

He edged closer. "Marc," he said quietly. "What are you doing? Serra's not due to wake up yet."

Marc's head tilted to one side. "*Picell nok draguul,*" he said. The skin around the turbine gem on his neck was dark and bruised. The one in his arm was the same. The implanted wires pushed at the underside of Marc's skin, creating shapes in the flesh. In his hand was one of the alien artifacts from the ship, a cylinder with a spike at the end of it.

Gafin's chest tightened. He moved closer, slowly, as though approaching a growling dog. "Marc, where's the captain? Where's Kam?"

A momentary frown flickered across the other man's face. He hesitated and his body turned, just a fraction. It was enough to pull Gafin's gaze. The captain was sprawled in the corner, an alien book cradled to his chest.

Gafin took a step forward. "Captain? You okay?"

Captain Kam nodded. "I'm fine." He tapped the book cover. "I figured it out."

"Figured what out?"

In the cryopod, Serra moaned.

Marc's lips twitched and he whispered the phrase again. "*Picell nok draguul.*" He lunged forward, burying the spike in her temple.

Gafin ran forward but it was too late.

Marc pulled the spike from his wife's skull and swung it at Gafin.

Gafin dodged but his foot slipped and he stumbled. His shin cracked against the side of the pod and he fell.

Marc stepped closer and raised the spike again. His teeth were bared.

"No!" Hennah screamed. She hurled one of the vials of medication from the shelf by the door. It struck Marc in the shoulder and he turned toward her instead.

"Marc, stop! Leave them alone." The captain's voice boomed like a detonation.

Marc froze. His black eyes blinked twice. The spike dropped from his fingers to clatter on the floor. He turned and strode from the room.

Gafin climbed to his feet. In the cryopod, Serra lay still. A trickle of blood ran from her temple into her blond hair. She was dead.

He swallowed the vile taste in his mouth and turned away.

"She'll be okay," the captain said. He tapped the book again. Its cover was dark brown leather, inlaid with alien script in some kind of silver metallic substance that gave off a faint phosphorescent glow. "This can heal her."

Gafin stared. "What?"

Kam already had it open. The pages were covered with the alien text, the symbols almost melted into the page, like the glitches that had been showing up on the computer screen.

"Honey, there's no way a book can heal a spike through the brain," Hennah said. "Even if that technology exists, we haven't found it."

He grinned. "That's just it. This isn't just technology. It's more...like a grimoire. I translated it. You saw how much better I made Marc with it."

"Better?" Gafin's fingernails dug into his palms. "The man stabbed his wife in the head. He's brain damaged. This is exactly why we were keeping him in hibernation."

The captain shook his head. "You'll see. Listen." He traced his finger over the page and chanted. "*Picell nok draguul. Picell nok draguul. Picell nok draguul.*"

Gafin exchanged a look with Hennah. It was one thing to have a captain who was obsessed with the technology to the exclusion of taking active command or paying attention to his wife – it was another to believe in alien magic. "Captain…"

Then Serra sat up.

An hour later, Gafin had run every test he could think of on Serra. He and Hennah poured over the results together. The damage from the spike was extensive.

"Brain activity is minimal. Frontal lobe and decision making areas are virtually non-existent. But she's alive and…she shouldn't be."

Hennah chewed her lip. "Do you think it will heal?"

Gafin shrugged. "I don't know. I wouldn't have thought so."

"Do you think Kam's right? The book brought her back?"

He stared at the puncture in his patient's temple. Serra sat still and silent. Her turbine gem implants had bruising around them like Marc's - invading the implants and the surrounding flesh, pushing on the underside of her skin.

"Something did." He pressed the communicator implant in the back of his jaw. "Captain, have you had any luck finding Marc?"

The response was a static hiss. *"Picell nok draguul."* Somehow the phrase had been recorded into the communication system. It was all it would say now.

"Computer, locate Captain Kam."

The screen was covered in symbols from the book. It was hard to read anything.

Serra's head lifted. *"Picell nok draguul."*

"That's creepy," Hennah said.

Gafin nodded. "I wish I knew what it meant."

"You don't think it's a healing spell then?"

He looked at her. "Do you believe in spells?"

She sighed. "I believe my husband should be more careful with the technology we find. I can't believe he actually used it on Marc."

Gafin touched her arm. Kam should never have been made a captain. He was a genius at deciphering the use of technology but being in charge required more than obsession and technical skill.

"I should go and talk to him." She nodded towards the computer screen. "The translation programme should be finished soon. See if you can get the computer to speed it up. We need to know what that book is saying."

Gafin handed her a hyperdermic loaded with sedative. "Be careful. If you see Marc, don't hesitate to use this."

Once she was gone, Gafin settled down at the computer terminal. The alien symbols on the monitor were like squashed insects on a windscreen. He switched it off and back on again, hoping to clear it.

He tapped the keyboard, then pressed the implant in his wrist up against the interface. "Computer, shut down all unnecessary functions and prioritise translation protocol. Translation required: *Picell nok draguul*."

The computer beeped in acknowledgement. The lights flickered and the ship gave a shudder as power rerouted. A few moments later it chimed again. *Translation identified by Captain Kam Nisholm. Picell nok draguul – Loyalty by obedience.*

Gafin frowned. "That was nothing like what the captain had claimed. Computer, check scans of alien artefact containing the phrase *Picell nok draguul.* Translate. What is the purpose of this book?"

The screen filled with text:

Cannot comply. Medical alert. Crew storage chamber unlocked. Cryogenic dehibernation sequence active: Pod 17; Pod 15; Pod 16; Pod 14; Pod 13; Pod 12; Pod 11; Pod 10; Pod 9; Pod 8; Pod 7; Pod 6; Pod 5; Pod 4.

The text flickered and blurred, letters converting to alien symbols and back again.

Gafin swore. That was all of the cryopods containing crew members. There was no way to safely bring more than two people out of hibernation at a time. To release them all at once strained the power supply and risked brain damage.

"Loyalty by obedience." The words cut into him like a spike to the brain. What if that was the point? What if the book was a form of hypnosis? Some kind of animating force that controlled a person completely? The phrase couldn't be enough on its own, could it? Unless that was what the spike was for. Marc had already been brain damaged when he was influenced but Serra had the control functions of her brain destroyed.

If the captain had opened all the cyropods then every crew member was at risk but himself and Hennah.

Hennah.

He ran for the cryochamber.

The voices reached him even before he made it to the door. "*Picell nok draguul. Picell nok draguul.*"

The pods were all open, spilling cold mist out across the chamber floor. Each one held a member of the crew, vulnerable, waking, helpless. Some chanting.

The captain moved between the pods, the cursed book in one hand, the cylinder and its spike in the other. He paused at another pod and stabbed down with the spike. Another voice was added to the chant.

"Captain, no!" The ship lurched and Gafin stumbled into the room, bile in his throat. "What are you doing?"

A hand reached out and grabbed his wrist, tight as a docking clamp. It was Hennah. A trickle of blood ran down from her temple. The turbine gem at her neck was black and bruised. Her lips moved but Gafin could only hear ringing in his ears. "*Picell nok draguul.*"

"Kam, what have you done? She's your wife!"

The captain paused. The chanting stopped. "I have done what I needed to do all along, Gafin. I have secured loyalty for myself and my position. You think I don't know you all laugh about me being captain behind my back? You think I don't know you're sleeping with my wife? She wasn't mine. Not really. But she is now. They all are."

Gafin struggled but Hennah's grip was too strong. "It's the book, Kam. The book is controlling you. It's corrupted your mind. It's screwing with the ship's systems. It's in our implants somehow."

The captain smiled. "It's not in my implants. And not in yours. Not yet anyway. But soon. Soon you'll do what I say, just like they do."

He advanced on Gafin, the spike raised and the book held out like a hymnal. "*Picell nok draguul*, Gafin. *Picell nok draguul.*" He swung the spike.

Gafin twisted, pulling Hennah off her feet and she stumbled into her husband. The three of them fell in a heap. The book and spike both toppled from Kam's grip, skidding across the floor.

The captain swore. "Get off me."

Hennah obeyed, letting go of Gafin's wrist to roll away.

Gafin rolled too, snatching up the book. He slammed it shut. The symbols on the cover glowed white.

"Give it back, Gafin. Everyone else on this ship will obey me without question. What do you think I'll tell them to do to you if you cross me again?"

Gafin stood up. Hennah lay still against the wall. Her eyes were open but there was no life in them. "There's nothing you could do that would be worse than what you've already done."

The captain followed his gaze. "I could give her to you. Give me back the grimoire and I'll tell her to be yours."

"She doesn't belong to either of us," Gafin said. "No one does."

He dropped the book into the nearest cryopod and shut the lid. He hit the control and the pod flooded with icy gas.

"No!" Kam ran at him and shoved him away, pulling open the lid. He reached through the gas screeching in agony as the icy temperature burned his skin. He pulled out his hands, covered in frost, frozen solid, the book glued to his skin by the cold. "*Picell nok draguul*," he gasped. "You are mine."

Gafin swallowed, stepping back in shock. "You don't control anyone," he said. "The book controls you."

"It's mine," whimpered the captain. "All of you

have to obey me. You'll be loyal now. Hennah will be loyal."

Gafin picked up the spike and brought it down hard on the grimoire. It shattered, taking Kam's frozen hands with it, red chunks on the metal floor.

The book screamed with the voices of the crew as they fell.

The journey home was a long one. Gafin travelled it alone. He sealed the corpses in the cryogenic chamber. He couldn't face hibernation any more. The ghosts on the ship would haunt him in his sleep.

The computer system was still infected with the alien programming, even after destroying the grimoire. It was impossible to use now, the alien symbols were all it would show and the translation programme was gone.

He was the only one alive. The captain had bled out when his wrists thawed and Gafin let him die. He'd murdered the woman they both loved and every other crew member on the ship. It was better than he deserved.

At last, he recognised the proximity alarm that indicated a docking procedure had begun. The ship shuddered as it landed. The computer powered down.

Gafin struggled into an envirosuit and made it to the door. When he looked out at the world beyond, his heart sank. Shelves lined with leather bound grimoires stretched in every direction like veins from a turbine gem.

This wasn't home. This was an alien planet. Worse than that, it was a library.

A different kind of zombie in "Loyalty". I originally wrote this as taking place in a traditional fantasy setting but it felt a little too obvious. Then I saw something online about jewellery designed to generate power from the wearer's blood flow. I incorporated something similar into a sci-fi setting and the cursed book became a kind of alien technology.

RECESSION

The reminder pops up on my screen. Seven thirty-five pm. Time for monster-check.

I click "snooze" again and finish typing my email. It has to be worded just right. Enough pressure to inspire action without seeming desperate. Enough confidence to seem reliable, without obvious over-selling. People are cautious with their investments in a recession. The economy can be a bitch.

I hesitate with the mouse pointer over the "send" button, then save it to drafts instead. I'll look at it again later. Maybe in the morning. The weekend will give it time to settle. I push the lid of my laptop closed. The whir of the machine slows and falls silent.

"Daddy?" The small voice comes to me from down the hall, a wisp on the air currents pushed out by the swish heat pump we had installed almost two years ago. Just before everything went South.

"Coming, Madsy." I close the door to the office. My wife is in the hall, a glittering black cocktail dress draped over her arm.

"For God's sake, don't call her that. You know I hate it. Her name is Madison."

I lean in to give her a quick kiss. "I know, beloved. Just habit."

The little lines between her brows crinkle, almost cracking her carefully applied makeup. "That's what I'm afraid of." She gestures at me with the dress. "Don't take all night in there. We don't want to be late."

I smile. "Fashionably."

"Hmm. Not too fashionably."

The door to our daughter's room is open. She never sleeps with it closed. I pause on the threshold to trace the design carved into either side of the doorway.

Madison peers at me from beneath a pink Disney princess duvet. Her hair is natural gold curls in a way that takes her mother hours at an expensive salon to achieve. A pity they can't trade.

"Daddy, you're late."

I sit beside her on the bed and stroke her curls. "Well, I'm here now. Did Mummy read your story?"

Madison wriggles under the covers, shifting onto her side. "Yes, but she read it too fast."

"Well, that's what you get when you take too long brushing teeth and getting into PJs."

More wriggling. "I didn't!"

"Okay, well, it's time to go to sleep now. I'll check the closet and under the bed for monsters and then it's lights out."

Madison goes very still. "You don't have to."

I freeze, already bent over to look under the bed, like a dollar bill folded and ready for the wallet. "What do you mean, Madsy?"

The nightly monster check is part of our bed time ritual. There's not much I can give her these days, but the security of a father who can chase away childhood fears is one.

Her voice is very small, emanating from the pink confection that is her duvet. "There won't be any monsters tonight. The lady will be here soon and she doesn't let them come."

I sit up and pull the duvet back from her face. Her eyes are very wide. "What lady, Madsy?"

Her thumb finds its way to her lips, almost blocking the whispered words. "The dead lady."

I form the words, but I'm numb. There's a kind of ringing in my ears. "The dead lady?"

Madison nods and pulls her thumb from her mouth just long enough to answer. "She stands in the doorway. The monsters are scared of her."

"How do you know she's dead?"

Madison shrugs. "She just is."

I'm shaking as I step into the hall. For once Madison makes no protest when I shut her bedroom door. I take a deep breath. My little girl is afraid of a dead lady she sees in her bedroom doorway. There are no suggestions in the parenting manuals for this. It's not something you can ask grandparents or friends about. Well, not without judgement, anyway.

I lean against the wall for a moment. Perhaps we should stay home tonight. The thought of it brings tightness to my chest. I can barely breathe. There are only so many of these wine and dine schmooze-fests at this time of year. If I'm not there to impress potential clients, someone else will. I close my eyes and can see the smug smile on Mark McGroady's face as he gloats about how he snatched up all the potential clients like a bully at a lolly-scramble and I missed out. The bastard.

I sigh. I need those investors.

I push myself away from the wall and make my way to the bedroom. Allison is dressed and ready now. She's a vision, her hair curled and held back at the sides with glittering jewelled pins. I know they're the same pins she's worn to a couple of these things already and she will be self-conscious about it, but the gems are real and wealth inspires confidence in investors. Well, the appearance of wealth anyway.

She's laid my suit and tie on the bed ready for me to change. I haven't had a new suit in two years. It's pilled, just a bit, at the back of the collar.

I finger the sleeve. "I'm worried about Madison."

"Why?" Allison looks up from lighting a candle. She has laid several of them around the room. It would have been romantic if not for the pentagram and the bowl made of bone.

"I just…" My voice drifts off. I'm not sure what to say. How to explain it. "Maybe we should get a proper babysitter this time. A real one."

Allison snorts. "And where do you think we'll find a reliable, live babysitter at this time of night?" She upends the bowl and spreads grave dirt onto the carpet. "Besides, babysitters are expensive."

I sigh. "I suppose you're right." I pick up the athame and prick my finger with it. A few drops of blood and the summoning is begun. I'm sure once more won't hurt.

"Recession" was written for the popular horror anthology, "Baby Teeth – Bite Sized Tales of Terror". The collection is a series of stories inspired by the creepy things children say and the proceeds went to a children's literacy charity. Recession was based on the childhood experience of a friend of mine who claimed he remembered seeing ghosts as a child – one in the doorway keeping another from entering his room.

"Baby Teeth" is available on Amazon.com and the anthology won a Sir Julius Vogel Award in 2014.

Slippery Road

The first time my dad died it was raining. Not heavy rain, but that light mist in the darkness that comes when the real rain is pausing and every breath pulls in tiny droplets to the back of your throat. I remember the car headlights reflecting on the wet road as he drove away, just like they do now, and Mum screaming and the smell of her cigarette.

"He's a deadbeat," Auntie told me then. "And dead to us now. Mind you don't grow up to be a good-for-nothing and abandon your family just like him. Useless."

That was years ago now, but I sometimes think of it when I'm in that sort of rain. It's not worth having a brolly, but if you don't carry one you know it'll bucket down half way home. Mrs Patel lends me one and I promise to bring it back tomorrow. "Mind you do," she says. "And try to get in early – there's two bins of Pacific Rose coming in and I'll need you to bag them all."

School finishes the same time every day so I don't know how she expects me to get there early. Maybe Auntie has been at her again to give me more hours. The deal was I could do year 13 as long as I worked every night after school but she still complains. It's hard to run a family with not much income these days.

Car lights reflect on the wet road as I ride my board down the footpath. Exhaust fumes mix with the scent of rain. It's almost nine. Auntie won't be back from her cleaning job until ten – that's if she doesn't stop at the pokies – so when I get to the park, I pick up my board and walk in.

The park has trees and grass or whatever for people to take their dogs for a shit then sit and picnic in it – and a half-pipe and some ramps. At this time of night there's no one else there so I have the whole thing to myself.

Everything's wet - not great for skating - but I need time to think. I drop my bag and the umbrella, climb to the top of one of the ramps, and step onto my board. Next thing, the wind is rushing past as I roll down the slope and head for the next one. The rain has stopped and I like the spray kicked up by my wheels. I ride up the next ramp, a short one, and fly over the hump, landing on the other side. The wheels slip a little in the wet, but I'm braced for it and adjust. Skids aren't so bad if you know they're coming. I use the extra momentum to get closer to a low wall, flick the board with my foot and do an ollie. A good landing. I kick off again and head for the half-pipe.

A hospital calling with a message from my dad – I didn't see that coming. Leukaemia with just a few days left, they said. And he wants to see me. After all this time. I don't know how to brace for that slide.

As I start the roll up one side of the half-pipe, I think back. My dad has never seen me skate. That's how long ago he left. As my speed picks up, I go higher and higher on each rise of the half-pipe, my board airborne for long moments. I ride it, flip it, pulling tricks that would wow an audience. I wonder what he would think if he could see what I can do with my board. How I fly with it.

Just last week some rich kid came up after seeing me skate and showed me a competition in his skater mag. It was national coverage and decent prize money and he thought I should enter. I grin, thinking about that. Me, a professional skater. That'd be sweet. I wonder what my dad would think of that. I pull an airborne twist and imagine I'm at the comp, Dad watching me in the crowd.

Auntie's voice scoffs in my head. "Get real – he wouldn't care."

My wheels hit the ground and skid in the wet again. This time, I don't recover. I'm good, but not that good. I hit the half-pipe with my ass and slide to the bottom. So much for showing off.

I get up, brush the water off my pants, and find my board. I step on the tail and it flicks into my hand. My dad isn't watching me skate and he never will. Not even if I do go see him in the hospital.

I head to one of the lower ramps. In this wet weather I should keep it safe. It'd be dumb to crack my head doing tricks on a slippery slope.

That's when I see the old man watching me. He's close to a tree trunk, just out of reach of the one faded lamppost, as if he doesn't want to be seen. I know he does. He sees me looking back at him and steps forward just a little. He's wearing shorts, a hoodie and a cap on backwards – as if that's enough to hide his sagging skin and grey hair.

I pick up my board and walk towards him. He looks me up and down and licks his lips – about as blatant as you can get. I can't help sneering as I hold out my hand and rub my fingers with my thumb. Money? He nods and holds out thirty bucks. Whatever. That's thirty bucks Auntie doesn't know about. I take it. The dirty old fag drops to his knees and starts praying to my zipper and I'm thinking about what I can get with the money. A couple of skate mags, maybe. Or a tiny bit closer to a new board. Even the entry fee for that competition – nah, Auntie would never let me take that much time away from school and work.

When it's finished, he looks up at me, wiping slobber from his eager face, and says, "I'll give you a hundred to return the favour."

"Nah, mate, I'm good." I zip up, grab my stuff, and start to walk away.

"Come on – a fresh hundie in your pocket, dude. Easy money."

The slang sounds stupid in his mouth. I could just bash him and take the hundred. *That* would be easy money. I ignore him and keep walking, one hand in my pocket, fingering the thirty bucks. At least somebody liked watching me skate.

A light's on outside the kitchen window when I walk up the drive. There's no car in the carport which means Auntie's not home. Inside, my little brother, Dan, is already in bed so it's just Sarah and her friend

Michelle talking about boys or Paris Hilton or something. They stop their conversation when I walk in and stare at me like they just noticed I was stuck to their shoe.

I try not to scowl. "What?"

Sarah looks away and busies herself with putting her cup in the sink. There's the whole day's worth of dishes in there already that she hasn't washed. That'll probably be my job in the morning.

Michelle moves towards me and squeezes my arm gently. I frown –not because it's bad, but because it's weird. I've always thought she was kind of hot, just not as hot as she thinks she is. "There's been some news," she says. "About your dad."

"What? Is he worse?" I look at Sarah and she still doesn't meet my eyes.

"H-he died this afternoon. I'm sorry, man."

I shake my head. "Nah, they just said this morning it'd be a week. We only just found out he was sick."

"I guess they got it wrong."

I try to find something to say to that but I can't. Michelle puts her arm around me and guides me to the couch. Her hair smells of fruit shampoo. She sits next to me on the old throw-rug that covers the holes in the cushions and holds my hand until Sarah brings me a Milo. "Are you okay?"

I shrug. "Well, yeah. I mean, it's not like I'll miss him or anything. I never see him anyway, ya know?"

"I know. But he's your dad."

I realise I'm still holding my skateboard and put it on the floor. I nudge it with my foot and it rolls half under the couch.

After a minute, Michelle gets up and lets go of my hand. I miss the touch, but it's a relief to have lost it. She fidgets and looks at Sarah, then picks up the TV remote and hands it to me. "We'll give you some time alone," she says, herding Sarah down the hall. "Your auntie will be home soon."

There's some reality show on TV. I watch it but only really notice the credits at the end. Car lights flash through the crack in the drapes. The engine stops and the door opens and closes. Auntie's home.

She stands quiet for a moment and we just look at each other. She's still wearing her smock from her cleaning job but she's got a jacket over the top so it doesn't look like a uniform. She's let her hair down and kind of brushed it forward so the little bit of grey at her temples is covered. Her pink lipstick is smudged at the corner of her mouth.

Eventually she crosses the room and sits beside me. The smell of cigarettes comes with her. "Sarah told you about the call this afternoon?"

I nod. "I want to go to the funeral."

Auntie shakes her head. "We can't afford a trip to Wellington. Especially not now that we won't be getting child support payments from your dad any more." She pats me on the knee. "Everyone's going to have to pull their weight a bit more now. You're going to have to leave school and get a proper job."

"But Mum said -"

"Your mum won't be out for another six months at least and I have to make sure everything keeps running. Things are different now. You can't afford to be dreaming." She stands up and smiles down at me, one of those sappy, pitying smiles. "Go and get some sleep," she says. "You'll feel better in the morning."

I feel frozen. I can hardly make my voice work. "In a minute."

Auntie nods and walks away. I stay, staring at the floor in the darkness. The tears don't leave me, even though I feel them there. They stay inside, building pressure in my chest. I don't know what to do.

I sit there for what seems like it must be the whole night but the darkness never lets up. Rain tumbles over the house like gravel from a skidding wheel, then slowly turns to mist. I pull back the drapes and look out at the streetlights and the wet, slippery road. I decide.

When light finally trickles into the horizon, I'm already at the edge of town. I move quickly on my board when there's no traffic around. Now, though, cars are pouring into the roads and it's no longer safe for me to ride. But I don't care. I need them now.

I stick out my thumb and start walking. Hitchhiking to Wellington is cheaper than a bus or train and the fresh hundie in my pocket is for the skate competition. I don't know how I'll get there, but I will.

An SUV pulls up beside me and a man with thinning, dark hair winds down the window. The mist of rain has stopped. The sun inches into a clear sky. I get in the car.

"Slippery Road" won first place in one national short story competition and second place in another. Somewhat edgy and with some content for which parental guidance is advised, it came from an awareness of difficulties in life and how sometimes there are no good answers. I wanted this story to be haunting for the reader. And again, the loss of a father featured – one of my triggers! I'm particularly proud of the opening hook sentence.

THE INTERVIEW

He doesn't look dangerous. That's the problem. His dark brown hair is slightly too long and falls almost into his long-lashed, gentle eyes. When he smiles, you can't help thinking he hasn't a bad word for anyone. He doesn't smile much but, even unshaven and unwashed, there's a certain boy next door charm about him that's disarming.

He is dangerous. They don't lock you in a supernaturally reinforced cell at the Edgewood Asylum for nothing.

I press against the layer of unbreakable glass between us. The room he's in is padded. Cliché, but it serves the purpose. The fabric is grey, except for a few places where he's painted flowers and landscapes.

There is a food slot in one wall with an electronic lock. It opens into a reinforced cubicle which is sealed from the outside world before the cell flap is unlocked. There's a similar airlock-type system for the door – it will never be opened. This is probably the only facility capable of holding someone like him.

The idea of spending the future trapped in a place like this brings a sweaty dampness to my face. The encasement doesn't seem to bother him. To me, it is foreign and sick.

"Are you sure you want to go through with this?" His voice is only faintly muffled by the barrier between us.

I swallow, and nod vigorously. "Yes." I need to know how he got here. I need to make sense of it. To find some answers. "Tell me what it's like being a superhero."

His face takes on a wistful enthusiasm. "Honestly, at first it was incredibly cool." He chuckles and I can't help but smile too. "In the movies, people are always all angsty when they get their powers, you know? But that's bullshit. I mean, seriously, who wouldn't love having superpowers?"

"I always wished I could turn invisible," I say.

He grins. "Hell, you'd be a force to be reckoned with then. An invisible reporter – every story would be an exclusive!"

"Exactly!" Damn. I've let myself be fooled by his charm already. I look away from his smile to give myself a chance to recover. There are scrape marks around the cell door. He's been trying to escape. I turn my head before he catches me looking. "So…what did you do when you first discovered your powers?"

He shrugs. "I got excited. Got myself an untraceable cell-phone, registered with the local police, joined the online forums to try to find a mentor to show me the ropes."

"Did you find one?"

"Yeah. Two, really. Gregory Clarke was the one the system matched to me. You probably know him as Arcweld. He has a lot of firepower and is super strong. The police contact I made was Officer Rebecca Stanford. Every new superhero gets a police liaison." He smiles. "It's not all bat-signals these days."

I can't help chuckling. "Yeah, somehow I don't think the bad guys would wait around while they shine the light on the clouds."

The smile vanishes. "No. They don't."

He is very still for a long moment, still and silent. I take a deep breath and try to prompt him. "So Arcweld and Officer Stanford helped you find work?"

He blinks and glances at me, nodding. "Yeah. The kind of stuff you get involved in through the police is the stuff that keeps you interested in being a superhero, you know? Saving people, stopping crime. That's the good stuff. But it's the military work and private contracts that pay the bills. Cops are funded by the government and they don't pay. If you're lucky, the person you rescue will give you something out of gratitude but most people just kinda expect it, ya know? It's sort of a human decency thing to rescue someone if you can."

I lift my pen to my notebook without taking my eyes from his. "You like to do the right thing?"

"Of course. That's what being a superhero is about. That much, I always knew. The rest I had to learn on the job."

I raise an eyebrow. "Was that hard?"

He gives a wry laugh. "Sometimes. More of a culture shock, I guess. My first time at a crime scene I didn't have a clue what I was doing. I got lost so I was late getting there and it was already a mess when I arrived. The bad guy had dodged one of Arcweld's attacks and it took off the side of a bus – you can imagine the insurance nightmare that was – and people were screaming everywhere. It was…horrible."

I nod, thinking of my own first violent crime scene as a new reporter. It had been a murder, but nothing involving superpowers. "I can imagine."

He looks at me oddly. "Yes, I suppose you can."

For a moment, we are both lost in our blood memories. It is a shared kinship that shocks me; the bond of understanding between those who have witnessed unspeakable things.

"I did well that first day," he says at last. "I was able to put one of my spheres around the bad guy, trapping him, and another around a group of victims who were in danger of being burned. Nobody knew what my superpower was back then, so they were all surprised by what I could do."

My chest tightens as I hear the opportunity. "How is it that you do what you do? How does it work?"

There is no hesitation as he answers. "I don't know exactly." He shrugs and holds out his hand. A transparent sphere, about the size of a snow-globe, appears above his palm. "I create these. I can put them around anything and I can manipulate anything inside them. Size, weight, whatever – it all changes according to the sphere."

I force myself to breathe slowly, my eyes fixed on the manifestation of his power. "I heard it made you pretty unpopular with the bad guys. You were…difficult to escape from."

He smiles and the sphere swirls with colour. Green to orange to blue. "Yeah. After that first day, the other superheroes wanted me around a lot more! Things got . . . very busy."

The pen turns in my hand. "What was it like for you?"

"Once I got the hang of it, it was great. Greg and Becks pulled me in on whatever they could. It got pretty hectic. Ally, my girlfriend, used to say she saw me more on the news than she did in real life. I had a reputation for keeping the body-count low. Each member of the team had a role. Becks got the calls, let us know where to be and responded. Arcweld was the heavy artillery and I was the guy who kept people safe. Got innocents in a fire? I'm there to put a sphere around them to keep the flames and heat away. Collapsing building? I'll put the rubble in a sphere the size and weight of an apple. Bullet headed for you? A sphere will protect you."

The blunt end of my pen traces swirls across the paper. "Wasn't that a lot of pressure?"

"No, I can do it." He leans forward, intense, his hand twitching with his words. "If I get there in time, it's okay. My spheres are unbreakable. They can save people."

I hold the pen still. "Completely unbreakable?"

He stares at me for a moment. The sphere floating beside him expands to the size of a basketball, then contracts. "Do you want to know how strong they are? Really?"

I nod, not trusting myself to speak.

"They're strong enough to carry twelve foot statues out of Afghanistan before the government there knew they were gone. Did you know our army is collecting mystical relics from other countries? Arcweld's military contacts were apparently very eager to get their hands on me."

"What?"

The bitterness in his voice is overpowering. "Oh yes. They took me away from saving lives so I could be their little sneak-thief. Who else can get through customs carrying two ton national treasures in their hand-luggage?" He stares into the distance for a long time, silent. "That was the last time I did contract work."

I keep my voice quiet, gentle, safe. "How did people react to that?"

His gaze swings back to me, not quite meeting my eyes. "Not great. The military was very insistent. I kept saying no and Ally didn't understand why. The police work was even busier so I was out a lot but I didn't have the income any more. I tried getting a regular job but that didn't work. Eventually she left."

"That. . . must've been hard." I don't know what else to say.

He nods, the sphere bobbing softly alongside. "Yeah. Becks – Officer Stanford – helped me a lot. She got it. Ally didn't. How could I hang out with friends or hold down a regular job while people's lives were at risk? I couldn't. Not when I could save them. Becks would feed me more and more jobs to keep my mind off things. We saved a lot of people, I think. But there's always more."

I stare at the marks on my notebook. Time seems too short and I don't have what I need. I don't have enough information yet. "There's always more," I murmur.

"Yes! So many more." He leans forward, on the edge of his seat, and the sphere rotates around him. "Everything depended on getting there in time. I'm not super fast. If I had been, then I could have saved her."

My eyes flick from his face to the sphere beside him and back. "Save who?"

He shifts back in the chair and plucks at the asylum issue grey shirt. When he speaks again it is with a flat, dead tone. "It was a bomb... in a packed shopping mall. Becks was trying to dismantle it but there wasn't time. It was already exploding when I reached out and... she was too close." He closes his eyes. The sphere pales to transparent, unbreakable glass and sinks slowly to his knee.

"You put the sphere around them both." My hand grips the pen so hard I can feel the imprint of it against my palm. I swallow. My heartbeat is loud and fast. "She died in the explosion. And the sphere still didn't break?"

His eyes open. The lashes are still long, but the gentleness beneath them is lost. The sphere at his knee rises to brush his face like a caress. "She died and I finally figured out how to keep the innocent safe." He smiles, but there's no humour in it. He waves his hand and the sphere at his shoulder disappears.

I lurch forward, notebook and pen tumbling from my fingers as I peer into the room, searching for some hint, some clue. "How did you do that? How do you make them disappear?"

He sighs and gets to his feet. "I think the time for

interviews is over."

"No, wait. Not yet! Please, tell me more about the spheres!" My fingers scratch at the smooth barrier between us.

"Ssh," he murmurs, and I'm lifted up in his hand. The glass swirls with colour: green to orange to blue. "You're safe in there. You'll always be safe."

I'm still trapped. Still helpless. He places my sphere back on the shelf with the others.

I originally thought "The Interview" might need to be a sort of video blog performance piece and I asked a friend of mine about how to create a special effect for the twist at the end. But after thinking it through a little more, decided I could make it work as a short story.

It was published in Andromeda Spaceways Inflight Magazine, was a finalist for the Sir Julius Vogel Awards, and later appeared in Obscured Vision.

AUTHOR'S NOTE

Thank you for taking the time to read my book. I really hope you enjoyed reading it as much as I enjoyed creating it.

Please consider posting a customer review and telling your friends about this book. Word of mouth makes a huge difference to an author and is greatly appreciated.

For special offers, release dates, and more sent directly to you, join my Readers Group via my website www.darian-smith.com

If you'd like to read more from me now, check out my novel, *Currents of* Change. I've included the first couple of chapters on the next page.

ABOUT THE AUTHOR

Darian Smith lives in Auckland, New Zealand with his wife (who also writes) and their Siamese cat (who doesn't).

By day, he works with people who have neuromuscular conditions such as muscular dystrophy or charcot marie tooth disease. He is also a qualified counsellor/family therapist and can be seen – by those very swift with the pause button – on television shows such as Legend of the Seeker and Spartacus.

For more information about Darian and his upcoming work, please check out his website

Website: www.darian-smith.com

Facebook: DarianSmithAuthor

Twitter: @DarianWordSmith

See below for an excerpt from my novel – a suspenseful story of magic, secrets, a haunted house, and a touch of romance in rural New Zealand.

CURRENTS OF CHANGE

Sara's fingers gripped the wheel, convulsing on it like a live electrical wire. The speedometer crept higher. Five…ten…twenty kilometres over the speed limit.

Gorse, clay, and punga trees merged into a green and yellow blur at the edge of a road that was cut into the face of the hillside like a tar sealed scab on Mother Earth. A scar that would never heal on Papatuanuku's wild green skin.

She kept her eyes fixed on the road and her jaw clenched until the distracting buzz of her phone fell quiet and she could breathe again.

So much for silent mode. She should have switched the damn thing off.

She swallowed, relaxed her fingers, and eased her foot back off the pedal, just a bit. Just a tiny bit.

The car crested the top of the hill and began the descent into the valley below. For a moment she got a glimpse of farmland stretched out like a blanket and the blue sparkle of the sea beyond that. Then the trees rose up again and shadow covered the road.

She'd been driving for hours. Since well before dawn when even the city had an eerie, deserted feeling about it. It was a feeling that extended well into the bush and tiny country towns that were all she'd seen since lunch. She hoped it would be deserted enough.

The world had potential in it – like the ocean she had glimpsed in the distance. There was sunlight somewhere, and she could get to it now. She had to believe that. To cling to it. She would find what she needed soon. The sacrifice had been too great otherwise.

She flicked the switch on the door and the driver's side window slowly wound itself down to let in the wind. The cool air buffeted her hair and face, cleansing and free, until she was trembling with cold, but her skin tingled with exhilaration. She had done what she needed to do. She was free.

A light flashed on the side of the road, bright and startling.

"Shit!"

She hit the brakes but it was too late. She hadn't realised how quickly her speed had crept up again. She glanced in the rear-view mirror. Sure enough, a speed camera vehicle sat tucked into the trees like a spider waiting for her unwary flight.

"Damn it." What speed had she been going?

She flicked the switch again and the window wound its way up. Her skin warmed quickly. She should have known better. Her mind began working on ways she could hide what she had done – ways she could pay the fine and keep safe.

Then it struck her: she didn't have to. It wasn't her vehicle anyway and she was already safe.

Already safe! The words echoed in her mind like something forbidden. Like blaspheming the laws of nature. The absurdity of it fizzed in her like a chemical reaction and she found herself laughing. Laughing in great gulping breaths that tore at her insides, where she wasn't quite healed, and cramped her stomach with pain but somehow she couldn't stop. She pulled the car over to the side of the road and yanked on the handbrake while the shuddering mirth ripped through her body. Sobs mixed into the laughter and suddenly she found she was crying. Crying and shuddering like a madwoman. Insane.

She clutched at her hurting stomach and tried to slow the sobs. She pushed the emotions down, forcing air into her lungs, deep and even. In through the nose, out through the mouth. That's what the counsellor had told her. For once Sara was glad she'd been visited by the woman. No matter what she might have told the nurses and doctors when she'd left, at least this simple mantra seemed to help.

In through the nose, out through the mouth.

Breathe in. Breathe out.

She swallowed the last of the emotion down and closed her eyes for just a moment.

It wasn't far to go now. She was nearly there.

"Come on, Sara," she told herself, her voice little more than a whisper. "Sort your shit out."

Her stomach ached still and she wondered if she was bleeding. No point stopping to check now. She'd deal with it when she got to her destination. She put the car into gear and accelerated out onto the road.

An hour later, the town of Kowhiowhio was a blip on the highway, just north of the Bay of Islands. She hadn't found it on a map. Even her GPS had struggled, only giving her a nearby intersection of the highway. If she hadn't been given a description of what to look out for she'd have driven right past it.

Wide green paddocks gave way to a sudden burst of shops and houses, like paint drops spattered on green carpet. There was a petrol station, a pub, a convenience store with its familiar aproned grocer beckoning from the sign on the eaves, and a few others.

"Kowhiowhio Four Square," read the sign. This was the place.

Sara pulled over and parked the car. Her grandmother's words echoed in her head. "Once you get there, ask the locals. They'll know where it is. It's a bit of a town landmark."

She pushed the car door open and dragged her aching body out onto the footpath. A town this size couldn't have too many landmarks but even here it seemed strange for an empty old house to make the list. She put her hands on her hips and arched her back in a stretch. Her stomach still hurt but not as badly as she'd feared.

Straightening up, she tucked a strand of dark hair behind her ear, then reconsidered and pulled it forward again to hide her cheekbones. She glanced at her phone. The screen glowed with notifications of missed calls and text messages. She slipped it into her handbag and strode into the store.

The layout was similar to most country dairies, if a little larger than most. It likely served as the local supermarket – if such a word could be applied to a shop this size. To the left, an internal door connected to the fish and chip shop next door. On the right, a segregated booth held a sign proclaiming, "Nate's Electrical" and had spools of cable on a counter but no attendant. In the main section of the store, shelves ran in straight lines with a clear path to the checkout counter.

Sara paused to pick out a few items of food. She was going to have to eat while she was here, after all. Something quick and easy for tonight, and something for tomorrow's breakfast. She'd come back and do a proper, healthier shop in the morning. She couldn't face much more than that right now and anyway the doctor had told her to rest up. She tried not to imagine what he'd say if he knew she'd been driving all day.

She grabbed a couple of tins of spaghetti, some cereal and milk. Then, as an afterthought, picked up a vegetable and fruit juice concoction in a small glass bottle as her nod toward at least attempted nutrition. Her arms full, she made her way up to the counter.

A handsome man in his mid-thirties was talking to the shop clerk. He was tall and rugged with dark hair that was just a little too long and stubble across his strong jaw. He wore jeans, a polo shirt with "Nate's Electrical" embroidered on it, and a troubled expression.

"You don't think she's up for it?" he said.

The woman behind the counter shook her head, her black hair pulled back from her face in a ponytail that bobbed with the movement. She was a Maori woman in her early forties with a tribal band tattooed around her wrist. "She needs to learn responsibility first or you'll have trouble on your hands. I think you need to learn more about how little girls think. You're floundering. You have been ever since Em died."

"Actually, Moana, I think I've done pretty well."

"You would."

His jaw tightened, strength evident in the line of the muscles there. "Meaning?"

The woman opened to mouth to answer, then caught sight of Sara. She frowned. "Yes?"

Sara felt her face get hot. She lifted the groceries in her arms. "Sorry to interrupt."

The man turned away.

"No problem," the woman said, still eyeing Sara suspiciously, as though she'd intentionally been eavesdropping. "Haven't seen you before. You passing through?"

Sara dropped the items on the counter and watched as Moana scanned each one. "Actually, I'm going to be staying in town for a while. At the old O'Neill house. Do you know it?"

Moana set a tin of spaghetti down with a bang. "Are you serious?"

Sara licked her lips, her mouth suddenly dry. "Yeah. Why?"

The scanner beeped twice before the woman spoke again. "No one with half a brain goes there, girl. That's a bad place."

Sara felt her fingers curl into fists. "And why is that?"

"Just don't stay there. It's a run-down dump of a place anyway. Why would you want to live there?"

A range of answers ran through Sara's head.

Because it's my family home.

Because I have nowhere else to go.

Because this whole town is a run-down dump so what's the difference? At least no one will find me and I'll be safe.

She was tired – so tired – and sore inside and out. This day – this whole nightmare – had gone on long enough. Frustration turned into belligerence and before she could moderate it, the words spilled out of her mouth. "Well that's my business, isn't it?" She threw the money on the counter and picked up her bag of groceries. "Can you give me directions or not?"

Moana's jaw dropped.

It was the man who answered, an amused twinkle in his bright blue eyes. "Head north from here, take the first road on your left, then the third right. It's a gravel road, looks like a driveway. The O'Neill place is right at the end."

Sara forced herself to nod graciously. "Thank you." She turned on her heel and walked back to the car.

"Don't blame me if the ghosts come for you in the night," Moana's voice called out as she reached the door.

Sara felt the echo of her earlier hysteria bubbling in her chest. Ghosts were the least of her worries.

The house was practically a ruin. The paint was peeling and a few of the windows were cracked. The grass was as high as Sara's waist and barely parted to make way for the gravel driveway. Closer to the house, where there was once a garden, gorse and privet had conquered roses, their spiked skeletons brown and dead.

Wisteria crept up the right hand side of the house, up two stories and onto the roof.

The property backed onto rugged, native bush on one side, and an overgrown orchard on the other. The unsealed road had just two other homes on it, spread wide apart and in considerably better condition than this one. Bumping over the potholes, she'd wondered if the directions she'd been given had been wrong. But, at last, here she was.

Sara popped the boot of the car and lifted out her bags, one by one. It had taken almost a week to smuggle them out of the house. She'd used work, her grandmother, and even asked the community nurse to help.

She'd been so nervous for days, every muscle tight, her insides trembling. All it would have taken was for Greg to notice one little thing. To ask one tiny question. "Where's that jacket you always wear?" Or "Why don't you put on that dress I like?" Then her plans would have unravelled.

Her hand strayed to her belly, just for a moment, and the judgement threatened to overwhelm her. That her plans for freedom had been so fragile, that she had lived that way for so long, still ate at her soul like acid. The counsellor had told her she was brave for leaving but Sara knew different. She had only done it now because her cowardice had been shown up.

She shook off the emotion, refusing to give in to her tiredness or her tears. Not yet.

Taking the first of the bags, she made her way to the front door, the long grass scratching at her legs. Three steps led up to an old wooden veranda, then the front door. The key her grandmother had given her stuck at first. The lock was old and rusted. But at last it gave way and the door opened. Taking a deep breath, Sara stepped inside.

"This is the house where I grew up," her grandmother had told her, pressing the key into Sara's palm just a few days before. "It's not much, but it'll be a good place to hide out and get your bearings again."

Sara had felt the sharp edges of the key like a serrated knife. "I can't. I don't know anyone. I..."

The old woman shook her head. "You can. And you will. You know it's time."

The crisp rough sheets and antiseptic smell of the hospital room had mixed with the sweet fragrance of flowers in a sensory reminder of where she was and why. She lowered her hand to rest above her vacant womb. How could she stay when someone so much more helpless would not? "Yeah, I guess I do."

"Then go. He won't find you there."

The musty smell hit her like a wave as she stepped over the threshold. It was clear no one had lived here in decades. Sara had to admit her grandmother was right – no one would find her here. The locals even thought it was haunted, judging by what the woman in the store had said. Well, that was fine with Sara. She would fit right in – a ghost of her former self, haunted by her experiences.

The door led into a hallway, with a staircase at the far end. Doors opened at irregular intervals, left and right. Sara set down her bag and searched for a light switch.

There wasn't one.

"Oh, come on." She let the bag slide to the ground and checked again.

The windows let in the late afternoon sun but shadows in the house were building. She began exploring the rooms to the side of the hallway. They were of varying sizes and shapes, bedrooms, living rooms, dining room, kitchen with a large preparation surface and an ancient wood burning stove – but no fridge. Furniture was covered in dusty sheets and cobwebs were strung up like party streamers.

No light bulbs hung from the ceilings. No power sockets graced the walls.

"You've got to be kidding me. No power at all?" She felt the last of her energy sag from her body. A little voice in her mind told her she was stupid for having expected things to be easy. After all, why would the power be connected anyway when no one was living here? It was typical of the sort of stupid expectations she always had.

She knew that voice. Knew it well.

"Go home, Greg," she told it. "I don't listen to you anymore."

As if to make her a liar, her phone buzzed. She automatically pulled it out of her handbag to see who was calling.

It was him. She hit ignore and the screen flicked back to the list of missed calls and text messages.

She slid her finger over the screen and cycled through them all. She knew what they would say. She didn't need to hear it. She hovered over the screen, her resolve wavering. Perhaps she should listen. Just in case. If it was bad, well, she was far away now anyway.

She took a deep breath. Could she face listening to him right now? Did she owe it to him after their years together? After so much pain?

Just one then. To see what he knew.

Her finger dove downward but never reached the screen. To her surprise, the phone flickered and went black.

She shook it, and pressed the power button. Nothing. The battery was dead and with it the last of the electricity in the house.

Sara sighed and hurried outside to bring in the rest of her bags before the sun set completely and there was no more light.

It would be like camping, she decided. She would make up a bed on one of the couches in the living room and explore the rest of the house later. The spaghetti she'd bought would do just as well eaten cold, and tomorrow she would go into town and buy a gas burner to last until she could get electricity connected.

In the meantime, she was fine. She was safe and she was fine.

Despite the strange creaks of the house timber and the whistling of the wind in the trees outside, Sara felt she really was safer than she'd been in a long time.

As sleep crept in to claim her, another sound reached her ears. A strange, whispery voice calling her name.

Keen to read more? Get your copy of "Currents of Change" from Amazon or selected bookstores.